CHAPTER ONE

★

Dangerous Ground

It was a chilly afternoon but Yenene, my grandma, sat by the broken window in her rocking chair. It was the same place she'd been sitting when Jez and I had visited her last week – it was as though she hadn't moved. Over her shoulders she wore a black shawl, and her silky grey hair hung down to her waist. Dark, troubled eyes stared out from wizened, yellowish-green skin, rough as ogre hide.

'Told you not to be looking in so often,' she croaked.

I took off my hat, straightening the feather that stuck out from the side of the crown. 'Yup, you did, Grandma. And I told *you* I'll keep returning till you see sense and leave with me.'

'It's too dangerous for you to keep coming back

here, Will; there are big rock quakes every day now.'

'Exactly, Grandma, so all the more reason why it's time you were leaving. A broken window *this* week, what will it be *next* week? The roof caving in?'

She sighed, kicking back on the rocking chair that creaked like a pair of old sky-cowboy boots. 'Quakes'll blow over, you wait an' see.'

'You know that's not going to happen, Grandma. It's been six months since the High Sherriff said we *all* had to evacuate the western arm, and the quakes have only been getting worse. Pretty soon the whole arm's going to break away into the Wastelands, and if you don't come with me now, you'll be falling down there along with it.'

Grandma pulled her shawl tighter. 'Stuff and nonsense, boy. You listen to too many stories. I'm an elf, and Phoenix Creek's my home – and no high sheriff's going to order this elf to leave it. I'm telling you, like I've told you before, I'm not budging. High sheriff's making a lot of fuss over nothing.'

'It's not a lot of fuss, Grandma. All that illegal gold-mining's weakened the heart of the rock. Engineers say there's nothing they can do to save it. I know how you feel, I'm an elf too—'

With grateful acknowledgement to:
Carolyn Whitaker of London Independent Books,
Charlie Sheppard and Eloise King of Andersen
Press. Also to Dean Burke for working with me
in illustrating the Great West Rock map.

★ THE GREAT WEST ROCK ★

Mid-Rock City

Gung-Choux Village

Oretown

To Deadrock

The Wastelands

The West Woods

'Half-elf,' she corrected me.

'All right, I'm a half-elf, but I love this place just as much as you do, Grandma. Broke my heart to leave. But it just ain't safe to stay here any longer. You're the last living soul left here, Grandma, an' time's running out.'

But by now I knew I was wasting my breath. Her mouth was set, and she was rocking back and forth humming to herself like she'd forgotten I was even there. It was the same argument we'd been having for months and I felt like we were going round in circles.

'You hungry, ma'am? I'll make us some lunch,' a voice called from the kitchen. My friend Jez poked her head into the room. She'd obviously been listening and thought it was time to step in as I was getting nowhere with Grandma. 'I brought some stew; made it myself from an old dwarf recipe. Ma used to make it all the time. And I got some of that chokecherry pie you like,' she said, unpacking the basket of food she'd carried in with her.

Jez and I had met a year before when she'd helped me track down the man who murdered my pa. Jez was good in a fight and, apart from my horse Moonshine, she was the best friend I had on the whole of the Great West Rock. She worked in the fort kitchen in Mid-Rock City and usually gathered up as much food as she could when she knew we were visiting my grandma.

'You don't have to fuss with bringing so much, Jez,' Grandma smiled. 'It's very kind of you, though, cos I ain't got the heart to bake pies any more.'

'I like fussin'. Besides, with all the stores closed down in Oretown, there's nowhere for you to buy food.'

'Yes, what *have* you been eating?' I asked.

'I'm gettin' by just fine. Been on this rock for a long time, way before there was any stores parcelin' up food

4

they charge far too much money for. Tyrone an' you might've moved all the cattle and horses out east but you didn't pull up the vegetables or cut down the apple trees.'

But Grandma didn't look like she was getting by. She was thinner every time we visited.

'What if the roof *does* come down on top of you during a night quake, then what?'

Yenene directed a skinny arm through the air. 'This part of the ranch house is holding together just fine; testament to your pa's fine building work.' Pa had built most of Phoenix Creek with his bare hands, and he'd constructed it well, although like most of the buildings on the western arm, the quakes were starting to take their toll.

The ornament of the West Rock that Pa had carved out of a hunk of wood sat on a table by the fireplace and I lifted it up. I was always blown away by its detail: shaped like a cactus, two arms sprouted from the thick central trunk. On their flat tops my father had painstakingly carved little towns and villages:

Oretown on the western arm, Mid-Rock City on the trunk and Gung-Choux Village on the eastern arm. He'd even carved the rail track, coiling like a clattersnake all around the outside of the rock. I clasped my hand over the western arm as a chill slithered up my neck. The West Rock looked kind of crazy and lopsided without it.

The wind blew up dust and grit, which gusted inside the broken window Yenene sat by.

'Barn's nearly finished at the new ranch, Grandma. Tyrone and the others are doing a great job,' I commented. The new ranch on the eastern arm covered only half the area of Phoenix Creek but it was still a working ranch and we'd moved over a good herd of cattle and a corral full of horses. Tyrone, the foreman, and I, along with a few other farm hands, were responsible for the day-to-day running of the place.

'Oh.' She began rocking faster, and the chair and floorboards creaked louder.

'We've thought about calling it Phoenix Rise, in memory of this old place,' I told her. 'Tyrone is gonna cut a board to go up over the arch entrance but we wanted to ask you first.'

'Call it what you like, it's your ranch now.'

Yep, this was definitely shaping up to be a repeat of our last visit, with me talking about the new ranch and Yenene digging her heels in. And, just like the last time, I felt my face redden in frustration.

'It's your ranch too, Grandma; your cattle, your horses. You should be there. It isn't the same without you.'

She shook her head. 'I'm not moving, Will, I've told you. All this'll blow over soon enough and then folk will start movin' back to Oretown and the ranch lands. Some might even run into trouble getting their land back.'

'And what if it doesn't blow over?'

'Will,' she said, stroking my hand, 'it ain't like I've gone totally nuts. I keep my horse saddled when there's a spell of big quakes, so if it did get really bad I'd just fly off. Quit worrying about me, Grandson. I'm where I want to be.'

'When it gets really bad, you won't have time to fly off, Grandma. Besides, you could get hurt during the quake, or the horse could get injured or spooked and fly off, or . . .'

Jez brought lunch over and I stopped what I was saying. Grandma wasn't listening. She was too busy

looking at the beef and vegetable stew and chokecherry pie.

She ate it all hungrily. It was probably the first decent thing she'd eaten all week.

After a long silence Yenene grinned. 'Is Chief Red Feather still hoppin' a war dance over human folk stealin' his land?' She gestured to the *Dugtown Times* I'd brought her last time we'd visited. There'd been a front-page story all about the new settlers, of which I was one, and the land allocation near Gung-Choux Village.

'Uncle Crazy Wolf says the chief's none too happy 'bout the way some of the new settlers been acting, not sticking to the boundaries agreed in the land treaties,' I said.

It was a bit of a squeeze getting everyone from the western arm to settle on the eastern arm, and tempers had been fraying.

'I ain't surprised. Human settlers and native elves never did see eye to eye – apart from your ma and pa, of course.' I was what was sometimes referred to as a half-breed, although I hated that name. Made me feel like I didn't properly belong anywhere. My mother was an elf, but she died when I was a baby, and my pa was human. About the bravest, most honourable human that ever lived.

'I'm just glad not to be a part of it,' continued Yenene. 'Chief's sure got his work cut out now with a whole bunch o' ranchers showin' up on his doorstep.'

We'd almost finished eating when I heard the sound of a horse approaching. I looked through the broken window and saw Moonshine and Jez's horse stamp their hooves and neigh. A winged horse was trotting towards the ranch, mounted by a man wearing a neat blue and yellow uniform, a cap with a crossed-sabre emblem, and carrying both rifle and sabre – a sky cavalryman!

The sky cavalry are an army of brave soldiers under the command of the high sheriff, the ruler of the West Rock, who fly on highly trained winged horses. They are based in a fort in Mid-Rock City.

'Soldier's coming,' I reported.

'Ain't he got nothin' better to do? He was here not that long ago,' Yenene grumbled.

Dismounting, the soldier tied up his horse alongside Moonshine then strode into the ranch house.

'Something smells good.' The soldier lifted the pot of stew off the stove and with the wooden spoon Jez had used to stir it, he took a mouthful.

'Hey, I was saving that for Yenene!' Jez protested.

'She ain't gonna need it, she's leaving.'

'I ain't going nowhere,' Yenene hissed from her rocking chair.

'High Sheriff's orders are that the evacuation be completed by today no exceptions. From now on, you're breaking the law.' He set the stew back onto the stove.

'Since when is there a law against living in your own home?' Yenene fumed. 'Besides, why does the high sheriff care if I choose to go down with the rock? Won't be him gets buried under a mountain of rubble.'

The soldier sighed, pointing the wooden spoon at us. 'Who are you kids?'

'I'm Will Gallows. This is my grandma.'

'And I'm Jez, a friend of the family.'

'What are you doing here?'

'Same as you,' I explained, 'trying to persuade my grandma to leave.'

'Then, like me, you probably figured you're

wasting your time.'
He looked at Grandma.
'Told me last time you'd
start packing.'

'And I did.' She gestured
to a couple of wooden boxes
over near the kitchen. 'I packed
some stuff from the barn before
it collapsed.'

'If I thought you were playing
games with me, ma'am, I'd
arrest you right now and take
you to the high sheriff in handcuffs.'

Yenene glowered at him. 'You're the one who's
playing games. Why don't you spill the beans and tell
us why you really want me outta here?'

Sneaking another mouthful of the stew, the soldier
took out a handkerchief, wiping his mouth. 'You're a
shrewd one, I'll say that for you – stubborn as a rock
mule, but shrewd. OK, then, I'll tell you. The high sheriff
was hoping you'd have moved over by now. See, we've
been having a few problems with the settlers on the
eastern arm. Some of the elf folk ain't too happy with

cattle roaming near their farmland. The high sheriff has been fair and just with the land allocations but there's still some ill feeling.'

'I knew there had to be something more to your little visits,' said Yenene. 'And how does an old elf woman figure in all this?'

'The high sheriff reckons that you coming to settle on the eastern arm in your new ranch would send out a good signal to the elf folk, being an elf yourself, ma'am, and a rancher too.'

'I get it. I shoulda known the high sheriff didn't really care about a crumbly ol' elf woman. Well, I ain't

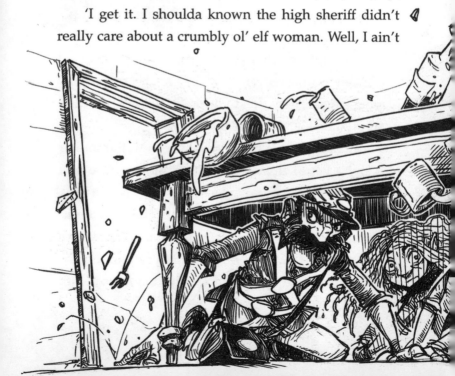

moving, not for you, not for the high sheriff, not for anybody. All you care about is making life easier for yourself. I ain't gonna do your job for you. Sort out your own mess . . .'

The first rock quake tremor was small, barely enough to rattle the pot of stew on the stove. But it was followed by a bigger jolt that made the floor jerk and had me staggering round the room like a newborn foal.

'Rock quake! Quick, everybody outside!' the soldier yelled.

'No time,' Yenene barked. 'C'mon, get under the table, it's big enough for all of us.'

We crawled under Grandma's kitchen table as the tremor worsened. Chairs and lamps toppled, bottles smashed, stew spilled, pots and pans were thrown from hooks on the wall of the kitchen to clatter onto the floor. Being from the western arm I'd grown up with the quakes, but it still didn't make me any less terrified when they struck. I clenched my teeth, feeling my heart race under my ribs.

And moments later, it was calm again.

Slowly we emerged from under the table. I made for the broken window to check on the horses. Moonshine whickered telling me she was OK.

Puffing out his reddened cheeks, the sky cavalryman dusted himself down. 'Gonna get myself killed comin' over here, and for what? Trying to reason with a crazy old elf woman.' He stooped to free his hat from under the fallen lamp stand. 'Well, if you're so determined to crumble into the Wastelands along with the rest of this spirit-forsaken place then go right ahead, ma'am.' And he shoved on his hat and made for the door.

'Wait, you can't just give up like this!' I called after him.

14

''Fraid I can, kid. I can't be wasting time riding over here any more. There's civil unrest a-brewing on the eastern arm and I'd be better served there, helping to finish the new fort by Gung-Choux Village. Fort's almost completed and I reckon the way things are shaping up we're gonna need it.'

'Huh, an' you've the nerve to come here asking me to move over there,' said Yenene. 'Sounds like I'd be whole lot safer staying right here.'

The soldier gasped. 'Already explained how you could be a help by moving to your new ranch, but you won't listen.' He put on his hat. 'I realise I'm probably wastin' my breath again, but before I go, I gotta warn you that on my way over here I chanced by a lone wolfer riding out near the woods. Mean-lookin' critter too.'

A wolfer is a professional wolf hunter. They kill wolves for their pelts so that the rich ladies of Mid-Rock City can wear fancy hats. When my pa was alive he warned me never to go near one.

'We can look after ourselves,' said Yenene.

The soldier headed for the door. 'I hope that's true, ma'am, cos I know for a fact they don't just stick to skinning wolves.'

We watched the soldier mount his horse then ride off in a cloud of dust.

Yenene turned to us and sighed. 'Maybe it's high time you both were going too, before another quake comes.'

'I'm not leaving you, not like this,' I insisted. 'Look at the state o' the place. I'm gonna help you tidy up then I reckon I'll stay here for the night. Can't help worrying about that wolfer the soldier spotted over by the woods, it's not that far from here.'

Jez nodded. 'I'll stay too. You'll need a hand, Will, and I don't have to be back at the fort till morning.'

Yenene rocked back and forth vigorously. 'If you think by staying you're gonna make me change my mind then you're mistaken.'

'We just wanna help,' I said. 'I'll go and stable Moonshine.'

'Ain't no stable,' said Yenene, 'it collapsed last week. I keep my horse out at the back of the ranch house.'

'I'll go tell Moonshine, then gather some logs to light the fire later. Reckon we're in for a chilly night.'

Watching us approach, Moonshine tossed her head, her white mane rippling in the breeze.

'We're staying for the night, Shy,' I told her. 'House is a mess, what with all the quakes of late, and it'll give us more time to try and persuade her to leave. Only thing is the stable's gone so you'll have to bed down out in the open with a blanket.'

'Stable? I don't need a stable,' she said, her voice soft. 'It's in my blood to be a hardy breed. When my pa was a sky cavalry horse he had to make do with wherever they were. Besides, I'd stand out all night in a tornado if there was a chance Yenene would change her mind and come with us.'

Most folk on the rock don't hold with talking to animals, saying that the Great Spirit created beasts to be submissive to folk and that they should be silent. But I am half elf, and elf folk have a bond with all animals. Critter chatter, as it's known on the rock, comes as naturally to me as herding cattle.

I gave Moonshine a rub behind the ears. 'I knew you'd be OK with it, Shy. But we'll need to be vigilant; sky cavalryman said he spotted a wolfer on his way over here.'

'I know, his horse was telling me while the soldier was inside talking to you.' She shuddered. 'Those smelly good-for-nothing wolfers give me the creeps. Why you would wanna do a job that involves having to cover yourself in wolf pee is a mystery to me.'

Jez strode over from checking her own horse and gave Moonshine a pat on the nose. 'Keep an eye on him for me, Shy,' she whispered. 'He's only a young 'un and ain't been outta the fort much, but I love him and the high sheriff says I can hold onto him for as long as I'm working at the fort.'

Moonshine raised up her head proudly then looked at me. 'Tell Jez I will. I'll keep a look out for trouble too. You can all rest easy – I can stay up all night if need be.'

I relayed this to Jez and she smiled. Then, fetching a couple of axes, we headed off in the direction of the collapsed wooden stable.

'One thing's for sure,' I said. 'There's no shortage of wood for the fire.'

CHAPTER TWO

★

Wolfer

That night a full moon rose over the West Rock, bathing the ranch lands in a pale ghostly light. Jez and I sat by the stone fireplace – blazing flames in the hearth – listening to Grandma snoring like a piglet with a full belly upstairs in her bedroom. Course, she'd never admit it but I think Grandma was secretly glad of the company. It felt strange being back in my old home again. I was getting used to the new ranch, and visiting Phoenix Creek always brought back old memories of Pa and growing up. It'd be sad having to leave again in the morning, and even sadder if Grandma didn't come with us.

Jez and I had worked hard all afternoon tidying up the ranch house: washing and drying pots and pans, picking up tables and chairs, hanging fallen pictures, fixing toppled lamps and setting back ornaments above the stone fireplace. Then we'd swept the floor.

Now I stared through the broken window at the full moon, hearing the rasp of crickets echoing – night noises. It reminded me of when Jez and I had camped out overnight on the side of the rock not too long ago.

'Reckon she'll come with us?' I asked my friend.

'Hope so, sure hate anything to happen to her. She's the closest thing to a real grandma I'll ever have.'

'I really appreciate you bringing the stew and all, Jez.'

'S'ok. I'm glad to be able to help.'

Just then Moonshine put her head in at the broken window. '*Pssst!* Will!'

'What is it, Shy?' I asked.

'We got us some company.'

My heart sank as one word speared through my head like a blowgun dart. *Wolfer!*

Lit by the full moon, a black horse rode towards the ranch house, mounted by a slight figure in a long cloak, wearing a wide-brimmed hat. As the trapper drew closer I could smell the stench of the fresh wolf pelts that hung from the saddle.

I opened the plank gun cabinet where I knew Yenene kept her rifle but was shocked to find it completely bare. I gasped, 'Spirits alive, the rifle's missing! Quick, Jez, help me look for it!'

We flew round the room, looking in cupboards and boxes, but there was no sign of it, and I could hear the horse getting closer.

'My bow and arrows,' I breathed and darted outside to Moonshine, plucking them from under the saddle.

Jez followed me, and when I looked round I saw that she wielded her little bone-handled knife.

'Should we wake Yenene?' she asked.

'No, we gotta protect her, don't even let on there's anyone staying here. Make out it's just us and we're leaving in a few days.'

The wolfer rode over to where we stood then pulled up.

'Well, now, what we got here?' Her voice sounded kind of weird, muffled, and, as the moonlight pulled her face from the darkness, I saw why. Below her wide-brimmed black hat stared two dark eyes, but the rest of her face was obscured behind dirty bandages. Her hands, as they clutched the reins, were bandaged too. I wasn't sure if she'd injured herself, if she was cold, or if this was some sort of weird wolfer disguise.

If the wolfer's masked face didn't make her stand out like a second nose, her smell did. I couldn't decide which smelled worse: the rotting animals hanging from her saddle, the sweat or the wolf pee. If she rode past a rotting carcass, the flies would probably follow her.

'By the look of those ears, reckon I've chanced upon a half-breed kid and his dwarf girlfriend,' she sneered. 'You two alone?'

'Yeah,' I fibbed.

She addressed Jez. 'If I had me a boyfriend and he brought me to a crumbling piece of rock like this, I think I'd ditch him pretty quickly.'

'Reckon there ain't much chance of you getting a boyfriend, ma'am, smelling the way you do.'

I nudged Jez. I figured getting the wolfer's back up would only make things worse, but I still couldn't help chuckling at her comment.

'Gotta smart mouth on ya, dwarf kid. No one insults me and walks away with skin on their bones.' Her long, dagger-sharp knife flashed in the moonlight.

And, with her other hand, she pulled out a rifle that had two of the fattest barrels I'd ever seen in my life. I felt the hairs on the back of my neck stand up as a chill ran down my spine.

'Your horse got some nice plump wings on her – fetch a good price from the twisted folks that live in the darkest parts o' the West Woods. Didn't skin me as many pelts as I'd have liked today, maybe I could make up for it.'

Moonshine pawed the ground with her hoof uncomfortably.

'Touch my horse and you'll regret it,' I spat.

'That's mighty big talk from an elf kid armed with a bow an' arrow, and a dwarf kid with the smallest knife I ever set eyes on.'

Just then a familiar voice rang out in the darkness, 'Look round or make a sudden move and I'll put more holes in ya than a big hunk o' Gung-Choux cheese. Now, throw down your weapons . . . real slow.' Yenene appeared from the gloom, rifle snug to her shoulder, aimed at the wolfer's back.

'Who says?' called the bandaged wolfer.

Yenene screamed like a demented coyote, firing

the rifle. Bullets tore through the darkness and took the trapper's wide-brimmed hat clean off her head and high into the air. An expression of fear flashed in the wolfer's eyes, and I chose that moment to raise the bow I was holding and shoot an arrow. It sliced through the air, embedding into the leather brim of the wolfer's hat as it fell from the sky.

'Next bullet goes through your head!' Yenene shouted. 'You're trespassing on my ranch.'

The wolfer watched the hat, now with built-in ventilation from rifle bullets and decorated with my arrow, fall onto the ground in front of her. Without her hat she looked even more grisly: a few strands of straggly black hair hung down to her shoulders. And in a gap between the filthy bandages I was sure I caught a glimpse of a green pointy ear not unlike my own.

The wolfer tossed down the knife and rifle.

'Ain't lookin' for trouble. I figured the horses were abandoned on account o' the evacuation.' She stole a glance at her captor. 'Did you say this is *your* ranch?'

'S'what I said,' Grandma snarled.

'Now I'm even more baffled. As if it weren't crazy enough an elf woman playin' rancher on the western arm, even crazier is the fact that you're still here, months after the evacuation order. What's the matter, you miss the last train, or somethin'?'

'Never missed no train, just like I never miss with this here rifle o' mine. Now, you can take your leave and see you don't hurry back, or next time you might not escape with your life.'

Picking it up, I tossed the wolfer her hat. She pulled out my arrow. 'Pretty impressive – first time I ever saw a cowboy shoot a bow and arrow.' Then she put the holed hat back on her head and galloped off.

When she'd left, Yenene turned to me, wide-eyed. 'Where *did* you learn to shoot an arrow like that?'

'Uncle Crazy Wolf's been teaching me some stuff.'

'He been teaching you about elf magic?' she probed, her eyes narrowing.

'Why would he? You said I can't do elf magic on account o' me only being half elf.'

'Cos he don't know any better, an' cos he sometimes forgets about the dangers of the dark side of the magic.'

I changed the subject as we watched the wolfer ride

off into the darkness. 'OK, now you have to come with us,' I said. 'That trigger-happy trapper will probably hang about like a bad smell then return sometime tomorrow.'

'Doubt it. She's already seen there's nothing to loot in this ol' place. Probably wouldn't have bothered me if she hadn't seen your horses. S'why I keep mine round the back.'

I couldn't believe my ears. 'So now it's *our* fault.'

'Ain't saying it's anybody's fault. S'just, I know how to handle myself. Can honestly say that's the first sniff o' trouble I've had in months.' She yawned and walked inside. 'I'm going back to bed.'

Jez and I followed. 'What about the wolfer?' I asked.

'By the look on her face, reckon that's the last we'll see or smell of her. Goodnight.'

That night I hardly slept for fear the wolfer would return. I sat in Grandma's rocking chair and listened to the crickets, keeping an ear out for the sound of a horse. I knew Moonshine would be too.

Jez curled up under the table. I told her there was another bed upstairs but she said the table reminded her of the little cavern she used to sleep inside on Pike's Ridge.

Whenever I closed my eyes I saw the wolfer's creepy bandaged face and felt a shiver chill my spine. But at least there were no more rock tremors, and eventually I drifted off to sleep.

★ ★ ★

The next morning I awoke to the smell of something mighty tasty cooking.

Jez was in the kitchen cooking breakfast: eggs and bacon and fried bread. Yenene came down when Jez called her and we all sat at the long wooden kitchen table. Nobody spoke much. Not even about the wolfer.

Taking a big mug of coffee and shuffling across to her rocking chair, Yenene said, 'Now, before you ask, I'm staying, and I don't really wanna go over it all again so don't waste your breath trying to persuade me. I'm still a bit tired after last night's little interruption.'

She shouldn't be, I thought, after the way I heard her snoring during the night.

'Just leave the dishes, and start gathering up your things. It's a perfect morning for flying so you should make the most of it.'

I could see it was pointless trying to talk her into leaving so I pulled on my boots. 'You're right, we'll get going.'

'I want you both to promise me you'll stay away for a while. Promise me, now.'

'I won't promise any such thing,' I said. 'We'll drop by next week, or maybe even sooner.'

'I'll bring you something real tasty from the fort kitchen, ma'am,' Jez added with a beaming smile.

Yenene said nothing but rocked and hummed again. Her muttering always got me mad and I turned to Jez. 'C'mon, let's go.'

Jez got up. 'I've left you some rice and sixberry pie. Pity you won't come with us. I'd sure hate anythin' to happen to ya, ma'am. You're the only grandma I got, if it's OK to call you grandma?'

Yenene looked at her and there was a flicker of a smile and a brief nod then more rocking and humming.

We left.

I saddled Moonshine. 'All set, Shy?'

'Where to, Will?'

'Home.' It sounded weird, especially as I was standing on my home – or what had been my home for so many years. 'Phoenix Rise,' I corrected.

Leaving Phoenix Creek, we flew over Oretown, just to see how it was holding together. Down below, I saw the main street with its rows of creaky wooden buildings: the mercantile store, the hotel and the

saloon that, like all the buildings
in Oretown, clustered together
like a line of drunk sky cowboys
trying to keep each other upright. But
it wasn't working, and in the face of the
harsh rock quakes many of them had collapsed. The
whole town had a strange look about it, with no folk
busily walking up and down its dusty streets any more.

As we flew over the sheriff's office, I thought of
its former resident, Sheriff Slugmarsh. He'd killed
my pa, his own deputy, a year and a half ago. But
I'd uncovered his loathsome deed, and now, after a

train-carriage-top accident, he was lying dead at the bottom of the West Rock. I hoped the next quake would flatten the sheriff's office too. Part of me was glad to be away from Oretown and the memories it held.

Soaring to the rock's edge, where we'd usually part company, I called, 'Thanks again, Jez, for helping me with Grandma.'

'No problem, just wish we could persuade her to leave.'

'We'll just have to keep trying.' I said. 'Wanna fly back with me? I was thinking of stopping off at Gung-Choux Village to see if uncle Crazy Wolf will teach me some more elf magic.'

'Can't, they'll be expecting me back at the fort. Though I'd love to see you do magic.'

My uncle Crazy Wolf, Grandma's brother, was the medicine mage of Gung-Choux Village. On first moving to the eastern arm, I'd plagued him to teach me some elf magic, and after a while he'd agreed. So, now, once a week, Tyrone gave me a break from my ranch chores and I visited my uncle. Yenene had always told me I couldn't do magic on account of me only being half elf. But then, while I was hunting for Pa's killer, I'd discovered that I did have the gift for magic and that Grandma had actually been protecting me from it. She'd been afraid I might be exposed to the bad side of elf magic. Elf magic can be a force for great good but it also has a darker side that I still didn't know very much about. All I knew was that, in the wrong hands, elf magic could be deadly.

I spotted the rail bridge in the distance and thought of something. 'Say, Jez, you wanna see something amazing just before you go? Won't take long.'

'Sure.'

'Great! C'mon.'

We flew up past the bridge, a shrill whistle coming from where the rail track spilled out of the tunnel.

'Flyer's coming!' I yelled.

The steam locomotive that was the Mid-Rock Flyer roared out of the tunnel like a fearsome, smoke-belching dragon. Great clouds of vapour spewed from its stack, while iron wheels clung to the bridge track like eagle talons on a tree branch. I noticed the worried faces of the passengers in the carriages.

The train driver hit full power and the Flyer picked up speed – no one wanted to spend a second more than was necessary on the stricken western arm. This was a dangerous place to be.

I urged Moonshine lower, heading close to the side of the Mid-Rock. Shiny new rail track was being laid around the outer edge.

'This is what I wanted to show you.'

It was the biggest rockside construction site I'd ever seen. A team of rail engineers, wearing safety harnesses attached to ropes, hung precariously, dangling off the rock face. Some carried long iron girders, while others waited to secure the girders into place on the side of the Mid-Rock. It was hot, hard work in the burning sun but humans, elves, dwarves and trolls all worked fearlessly together.

'Wow! What's going on?' Jez asked.

'The railroad company are thinking ahead. When the western arm collapses the rail track will give way with it, breaking the link to Deadrock and the Westwoods. So they're building a brand-new section of track that the company plans to join up sometime in the future.'

'Won't it get damaged during the collapse?'

'They reckon not. They say when the arm breaks away it'll fall outwards, kinda like a branch snapping off a tree.'

'They'd have to pay me plenty to do that job,' said Jez, glancing at a dwarf hanging perilously by a rope. 'When are they gonna divert it?'

'Soon. I heard they're putting extra men on it to get it finished. They don't reckon the western arm's got too much longer.'

As we flew in for a closer look the rock resonated with a low rumble.

'What was that?' Jez shrieked.

I felt my stomach lurch and said nothing.

'Sounded like a thunder dragon,' Jez went on.

'That's no thunder dragon. Quick, we gotta get outta here.'

We spurred the horses on and soared higher just as an all-powerful rock quake struck. Above us boulders big as ranch houses split off from the western arm, tumbling, like a stone waterfall, into the chasm. The noise was deafening. For a heart-stopping second I thought the whole arm of rock might break away before our eyes to crash on top of us.

'Look out, Will!' Jez cried.

A huge boulder plummeted past me, barely a horse's width away. I felt my heart judder against my ribcage.

Jez flew alongside me; her face now paler than Moonshine's hide. 'What are we gonna do?'

'We'll never make it to the top of the gorge; this boulder deluge is getting worse.' My eyes raked the rock face before I spotted something. 'Shy, ya think you could make it to that ridge? It's covered by a big outcrop, we'd be sheltered.'

'Yeah, I can make it,' Shy called back.

Darting between boulders, Moonshine swooped in closer to the ridge. Jez, black hair billowing out behind her, stuck like glue to Moonshine's tail.

In a flurry of wing beats we landed safely on the ridge.

'What if this breaks away?' Jez asked, dismounting.

I did the same, clutching the reins tightly. 'We'll have to risk it, it's our only chance.'

I stumbled on the shaky ground, struggling to keep my balance. The ridge was quite narrow and one powerful jerk could easily toss both of us into the canyon. The horses were distressed too, kicking, rearing and neighing loudly.

'This is all my fault!' I yelled above the noise of the crashing rocks. 'I shouldn't have brought you down here. You would have been halfway home by now.'

'It's not your fault,' Jez replied. 'I wanted to come. Besides, I wouldn't have got to see the new rail track an' all. I just hope Yenene's OK.'

And then, as quickly as it had come, the quake abated. The torrent of boulders ceased, to be replaced by a cloud of dust that rose from the canyon floor.

Taking off my hat to sweep back my fringe, I looked at Jez. She blew out her cheeks, running a sleeve over her forehead.

'*Pheeeyeeew!* S'all I can say.'

'Yeah, that was a biggy,' I panted, checking Moonshine's saddle and giving her a rub behind the ears. 'You OK, Shy? Best get going before another quake strikes.'

'Yeah.' Jez nodded.

We climbed upwards to the rock top then went our separate ways, Jez continuing to Mid-Rock City at the highest point of the rock, and me towards the eastern arm and Gung-Choux Village to see Uncle Crazy Wolf.

Jez waved furiously and, lifting my hat with my still trembling hand, I waved it back at her.

CHAPTER THREE

★

Guns and Magic

Gung-Choux Village, in spite of its name, was many times bigger than Oretown. But there were no wooden buildings clustering together like rows of drunk sky cowboys here. Instead, colourful tepees sprawled out over the lush green grass. The skin coverings of the elf homes were painted in bold greens, blues and yellows, patterned with triangles and circles. Some had more detailed animal shapes on, and a few even had scary designs: staring eyes or dagger-like teeth.

In the middle of the village, the tribal totem pole towered high in the sky. It was a magnificent structure, made up of man-height sections placed one on top of the other, each section painstakingly carved in the shape of an animal native to the West Rock: a frog, a pick-tooth wolf, a gutfish and an eagle. At the top sat the most impressive carving of them all – its dark eyes staring out over the whole of the eastern arm, its mouth clenched shut with two huge bottom canines protruding up past its nostrils – the head of a mighty thunder dragon. Thunder dragons are the biggest, most powerful creatures on the West Rock, though they mostly inhabit the less-populated areas of the Wastelands and West Woods. With long scaly bodies and sabre-sharp talons on their feet and wings, they hunt pick-tooth wolves and wasteland hyenas.

As a kid, when Yenene brought me to visit Uncle Crazy Wolf, I'd been terrified of this carving, and I used to spend most of the day hiding in his tepee.

It was now mid afternoon and I sat by a small fire in the centre of a cluster of tepees. I'd just finished painting my face with green stripes and was trying to study a leather-bound medicine mage book Crazy Wolf had given me entitled: *Medicine Magic for Healing Cuts and Burns*. But my attention kept wandering to two elf braves kneeling, fastening skins to the wooden frame of a long canoe. They were going fishing in the Gung River, and I started thinking how long it'd been since I'd last caught a nice fat gutfish.

My uncle came out of his tepee. He was bare-chested, his green skin painted with magic symbols in bold yellows and reds, and wore fringed buckskin leggings decorated with colourful beadwork. On his head was a band with a single feather that rose skyward like his long pointy ears. His face was adorned with two parallel white stripes, which denoted a medicine mage. They ran from cheek to cheek across the bridge of his nose. His grey hair hung in two long plaits, and he carried two wooden masks, a quiver full of arrows and two bows.

He smiled and handed me a bow. 'Come, little

warrior, you need a break from studying. Let's shoot a few arrows.'

I put down the book and followed him gladly, heading for an old gnarled tree on the edge of the village.

'So my pig-headed sister will not come,' he said as we walked. 'I am not surprised. Even when we were children playing together she could be very stubborn if she did not get her own way.'

'Maybe if you came next time she might listen.'

'Like she did back then? No, I can't see it making any difference. Once she has set her mind on something there's no moving her – she is like the West Rock in the most ferocious of tornadoes.'

I patted the carved wooden blowgun stuck in my belt. 'We could always frog poison her,' I laughed. I carried the blowgun everywhere with me, along with a jar of poison made from the sweat of the wood frog. A blowgun dart tipped with even a tiny bit of the poison would send its victim into a deep, delirious sleep.

It had saved my life more than a few times over the past year.

Uncle Crazy Wolf smiled. 'A bit drastic, Will, but I can't say it hasn't crossed my mind. It would be better if she came of her own accord. If we drag her to the new ranch kicking and screaming she will only be more bitter. I fear all this is because she has lost heart, and I just hope . . .' his voice trailed off.

'What?'

'I just hope in time she will find that heart again.'

'We don't *have* time. The rock isn't gonna wait until Grandma's made up her mind to move and *then* collapse. It's ready to break off at any moment. That quake I got caught in on the way over here was the biggest I've seen yet.'

My great-uncle looked skyward. 'These things we must leave with the Great Spirit. It is He who will decide what destiny holds for my sister.' Then he handed me an arrow saying, 'Conjure fire to the arrow tip.'

I took the arrow, cupping my hands around the tip, and began to concentrate. After a while smoke began to seep through my fingers. I blew softly then quickly moved my hand as a flame danced on the arrow tip.

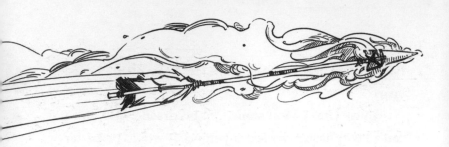

I was pleased with myself for working the magic so fast.

'Good. Now I want you to shoot the arrow and hit the centre of that tree.'

'No problem,' I said. We'd been practising this for weeks. I hadn't been a bad shot even before my uncle had started teaching me. But now, after learning from the best, I was much better.

Taking aim, I released the arrow. It whistled through the air, embedding into the soft trunk – direct hit! It was a saddlewood tree and saddlewood is quite magical too. When stripped of its bark, the wood gives off a soft purple light, bright enough to illuminate dark underground caves and mines. The underground city of Deadrock is lit almost entirely by saddlewood. Its other property is that it is resistant to fire, so my arrow flame soon died harmlessly away.

'Hmm, too easy for you.' Uncle Crazy Wolf took the bow and arrow from me. 'Maybe, since you mentioned it, we'll practise with your blowgun today.'

Opening the beaded pouch tied to my belt, I took out a blowgun dart – a splinter of river cane topped with the down of a fire-spitting eagle – and placed it in the mouthpiece end of the blowgun. Then I put the blowgun to my lips.

'Not so fast. We're going to try something a bit different today.'

He fetched one of the mage masks saying, 'Take off your hat.'

I did as I was told, and he placed the mage mask over my head.

I knew I wasn't supposed to but I put my cowboy hat back on, resting it on top of the mask.

Crazy Wolf laughed. 'Now you look ridiculous: a cowboy medicine mage.'

I stumbled around, bumping into a tree. 'I can't see a thing; there are no eye holes in this mask, Uncle.'

'I know. Now, hit the tree with your blowgun dart.'

'What?'

'You heard me, hit the tree.'

'But I can't s—'

'To a real mage that should not make any difference.'

I aimed at where I hoped the tree would be and blew sharply. I heard the dart whistle through the air. I didn't hear the dull thud it should've made as it embedded into the tree and knew I'd missed.

'No good,' said Crazy Wolf.

'I know.'

'But I did it back at Phoenix Rise with a bow and arrow when I hit the wolfer's hat in the darkness.'

'This is what worries me about you. You can do magic when under threat. This is when it is easy to succumb to the darker side of elf magic. Try again, only this time rely not on your judgement, instead reach out with your inner self. Travel with the dart, feel the wind rush over you. Sometimes we only think we see; we rely on our eyes so much we forget to work out what they tell us. With our eyes closed, and with a little magic, our minds can see so much more.'

I put the blowgun to my lips again. I pictured the middle of the tree in my head.

'Only let go when you trust the dart with not just your mind but also with your heart.'

Firstly I focused on the taste of the blowgun tip, then on the dart, reaching out with my consciousness.

A vision of the tree's bark began to form in my mind's eye, getting bigger; growing before my eyes, fading then becoming clearer. I let my arms be guided by the vision, aiming the blowgun first left then a little to the right then . . . shoot.

'Bull's-eye!'

I took off the mask and gasped. The dart was embedded right in the centre of the tree trunk.

'You learn quickly, young Will. I am very pleased. As I've told you before, there is an elf brave inside you bursting to get out.'

I heard distressed neighing behind me and spun round to see Moonshine, her head stuck in the other mage mask. The mask only partially covered her nose and she flung her head wildly from side to side trying to dislodge it. We both burst into fits of laughter as I went to help her.

'Now I've seen it all; first a cowboy medicine mage, now a horse medicine mage,' said my uncle.

We were still laughing when a group of real elf braves on horseback galloped over to us.

'Crazy Wolf, we need you over at the pass,' the leader said breathlessly.

'What is it?'

'Pale-skin settlers' cattle have overrun the corn fields, trampling all over it.'

'They're rooting out the buried corn stores too,' said another. 'Come quickly or we shall starve this winter.'

'I'll get my horse.' He turned to me. 'Will, you're an expert at rounding up cattle. Please ride with us – we could do with your help.'

'Of course, Uncle.'

The young brave looked at me. 'Thank you, now, come, there is no time to spare.'

Another few braves joined us on flightless rock ponies as we rode back through the village, and seven of us rode out at full gallop. Elf braves have no need of winged horses like Moonshine, preferring the strength and stamina of the rock pony for farm work and pulling carts.

We followed a course along the Gung River. Not far from the village we passed the new sky-cavalry fort, which looked almost complete. A few soldiers were finishing the top of one of the lookout towers, while others worked busily digging a trench.

I noticed the young brave gesture towards it with his spear, an angry expression on his face.

'They build a fort to keep law and order, so they say, but the truth is they build it to keep the elf down while pale-skin humans stride with their big cowboy boots all over elf land.'

'Like they did with our forefathers,' Crazy Wolf added.

Soon I could see the cattle in the distance. I guessed there were about twenty, roaming carelessly on, what to them, must've been a gold mine of tasty corn.

'OK, Shy, let's get this lot back to where they came from.'

'No problem.'

I rode Moonshine close to the herd, which began to moo and bellow.

The elf horses weren't used to cattle and appeared nervous.

I cantered up to Crazy Wolf. 'Tell 'em to walk their horses in slow, let them get used to the movement and smell of the steers, then they should be fine.'

He smiled then rode over to pass on the instruction to the other braves.

We worked together as a team, driving the cattle

gently off the corn fields. Some of the braves took to ranching quite well, but others were pretty hopeless and I had to step in when a few of the cattle broke loose and hurried back to their unlawful lunch.

'Whose brand is it?' asked one of the braves, referring to the identification mark burned onto the skin of the cattle so ranchers can tell which steers belong to them. 'Don't recognise it.'

I knew it only too well.

'I might've guessed – the Gatlans.'

'You know them?' The young brave asked.

'I heard Pa talk about them. Reckoned they were bad news. Pa said they stole some of his calves then burned their own brand on the hides, threatened to shoot Pa if he came near their land again.'

'Then I reckon they're bad news too. Your pa was a good judge of character, that's for sure.'

I smiled. 'He was. But I don't know where their ranch is so we'll just have to drive them on up the pass.'

We'd begun to steer the cattle along the plains, when a big, high-sided wagon pulled by a couple of black horses trundled towards us. Two men sat in the wagon seat. The bigger of the two, who held the reins, was a red-bearded giant of a man with a Boggart's-Breath filter moustache and jaws like a bear trap. The second man was skinny as a rifle barrel, with long legs (seemed like he was nothing but legs), a tanned face and sunken, staring eyes.

'Just what the heck do you think you're doin'?' the bigger bellied of the two men spat.

Uncle Crazy Wolf pulled up his horse alongside the wagon. 'Are these your cattle?'

'Sure are, and you got no call to be drivin' 'em anywhere.'

'I do when they're trespassing on our land, tramping all over our corn fields.' He raised his staff. 'I am Crazy Wolf, medicine mage of the Gung-Choux tribe, and these cattle were roaming on our land.'

'Buck Gatlan,' the fatter man introduced himself. 'An' my brother Whip. Well now, magic man, I don't see how you got more claim on that land than we have.'

'What you green skins gotta understand,' Whip added, 'is that we're in what you might call a changeover period since moving to this here part of the Rock, and it's gonna take time for proper treaties to be written up on the division of lands and who gets what, if you know what I mean.'

'I know very well what you mean, and you can be sure Chief Red Feather will not be oppressed into giving up any more land, especially when he has been more than generous already.'

'Generous?!' Buck rasped, the veins on his neck bulging. 'You call sweeping us into some little corner of the rock top with a handful of scorched grass, a bunch o' rollin' hills and a useless forest, generous? Heck we're ranchers; we need land to let the herd roam. Ain't right to coop up ranchers. Ain't just us, either, other ranchers been complainin' too.'

'What isn't right is letting your cattle graze on our land,' said Crazy Wolf firmly.

Whip had been staring at me for some time, and now he spoke, 'Say, you look like you got some rancher in you, kid. Never saw an elf with a painted face wear a sky-cowboy hat before, even though there's a feather stickin' out of it.'

'I'm not a kid,' I said. 'I work as a hand at the settlers' ranch over at Phoenix Rise. We're fencing our steers in and you should be doing the same.'

'Gotta big mouth on you, half-breed,' Whip raged. 'Nobody tells a Gatlan how to ranch their cattle, 'specially some half-breed.'

Reaching behind the wagon seat, the rancher lifted the biggest rifle I'd ever set eyes on. He handed it to his brother then stretched a second time for a similar weapon.

The braves shrugged bows off their shoulders and tugged arrows from quivers. Crazy Wolf raised the gnarled spear that most times he used as a walking stick.

The Gatlan brothers laughed. The big one drawled, 'You boys come at us with sticks when we got metal.'

'I think you better start showing us a little respect. You oughta know that humans are better than any elf, troll or goblin,' his brother added.

I felt my heart hammer like a war drum. I had a bad feeling about all this. I didn't like the way both sides were squaring up to each other.

'No one's better than anyone else on this rock,' I said.

'The young 'un is right,' said Crazy Wolf. 'The elf belief is that the Great Spirit created us all equal.

The elf seeks to live in harmony with his neighbour. I can speak to Chief Red Feather about arranging another meeting in Dugtown or in Gung-Choux Village. We could talk through our difficulties.'

'Talkin's all well and good but, see, it only really works if one side's willing to listen, and I get the distinct feeling you ain't willing to do that.'

'Not only that,' Buck added with a sneer, 'but I worry that you elves might not do what you're told, and if that was the case then we might just have to employ a little persuasion.' He tapped the butt of his rifle.

'Is that a threat?'

'Oh that ain't no threat, that's a promise.'

I stared at Buck's twitching mouth as it churned the bacca weed around. Every now and then when he had a mouthful of saliva he'd eject a huge gobbet of spit onto the ground. Only this time he directed the gobbet onto my uncle's face.

The elf braves moved forward on their horses, raising their weapons but Crazy Wolf stretched out his arms, staff in hand. 'Stop!' he cried. 'We will not play into their hands.'

My uncle took out a handkerchief and wiped his face. Then he stared at Buck.

'Hundreds of years ago men like you drove my ancestors off the western arm, slaughtering many innocents along the way. I intend to make sure that does not happen again and that the eastern arm remains elf country for ever.'

Buck was unmoved. 'In case you hadn't noticed, gentlemen, the Rock is crumblin'. Land's gettin' to be more precious than gold. An' what with the population growin' too, time's comin' when if a man wants land he's gonna have to fight for it. Us ranchers have formed a little committee and we're all agreed that somethin's gotta be done.'

As we were arguing, I noticed the lead steer, the one wearing a bell around its neck, had begun to amble back in the direction of the cornfields with the rest of the herd following – probably hoping we wouldn't notice them sneaking back to their feast.

'This bickering back and forth is getting us nowhere and your cattle need herding back to your ranch. We are willing to help. We will follow your wagon,' Uncle Crazy Wolf offered.

'We ain't goin' back to the ranch,' said Whip. 'We got us some business in the town o' Blackwater.

Leave them an' we'll ride out later an' bring them in.'

'After they've stripped our fields of every last ear of corn – this is outrageous, you will move them now!'

'Well there's no cause to get all shirty, ol' wizard,' Buck sneered. 'Say, what is all your medicine mumbo jumbo? Never did believe in any o' that stuff. I figure it's nothing more than a pile o' horse dung cowards use to frighten folk into leavin' 'em alone.'

'I have heard enough.' My uncle gestured to the other braves. 'Come. We will herd the cattle ourselves. But if they fall prey to wolves then their blood is on *your* hands not *ours*.'

Buck raised his weapon and let off two rounds into the air. The frightened cattle moved restlessly in the distance. 'Leave them be or I'll blow your head off.'

Crazy Wolf tucked his spear into his saddle. Reaching into a pocket, he removed some dried brown leaves, crushing them between his palms. As he did so, he muttered some words in the elf tongue. And slowly, very slowly, a ball of dark, cloud-like steam began to form above his hands, spinning furiously, whistling like a storm. The Gatlan brothers stared open mouthed. Their horses stirred uneasily, neighing loudly.

Whip, his voice quivering, sneered, 'What's this? You conjuring a little hocus pocus? Well, we ain't impressed.'

'Shut up, Whip,' snapped his brother. 'What the heck are you doin', elf?'

When the ball of wind was the size of a head, Crazy Wolf uttered a loud cry and it shot, bullet-quick, towards the Gatlans, who lurched forward, almost falling into their horses. At the last second, the ball veered to the right, blasting a large hole in the side of their wagon. With the noise of splintering wood, it tore through the wagon's cargo of wooden trunks and boxes to blow an exit hole through the far side. Even then it didn't stop. It circled the vehicle like a whirlwind, only inches from the Gatlans' bewildered faces, before again careering into the side of the wagon, peppering it with another hole. Finally it shot into the air, where it expanded to a huge black cloud, temporarily darkening the sky.

The noise of sharp claps of thunder was deafening as, spreading out, the cloud spat forks of lightning that reached down to dance across the ground. I saw the colour drain from both Buck and Whip's cheeks as they sat, totem pole still, staring at the sky.

My heart pounded relentlessly against my ribcage. I'd never seen this particular magic before. The nearest thing I'd seen my uncle conjure was a ball of fire when we were out fishing on Gung River once.

Whip grabbed his gun but Buck put a hand to the barrel, pushing it down. 'Hold your fire, Whip,' he said, probably as he'd noticed another wind ball begin to form in Crazy Wolf's palms.

'Reckon you're getting yourself a little worked up there, mister. Never saw nothin' like that before in my life. What do you call it?'

Crazy Wolf, not taking his eyes off his palms, said, 'A thunderball. It is powerful elf magic. Kill us now and it will still take both your heads off, as once conjured it must finish its magic or divert to the sky at my command.'

I saw Buck swallow a boulder-sized lump in his throat. He nudged Whip, who had already clambered

back into the cart seat, to give him a hand up. As he did I caught a glimpse of something shiny through the gaping hole in the side of the wagon. Edging Moonshine closer to the wagon, I peered inside. The force of the thunderball had blown the lids off some of the boxes, and neatly packed inside were rifles and ammunition. What would ranchers be doing with such a deadly cargo of weapons?

'We've wasted enough of our time here,' Buck grunted, 'we'll head back to the ranch and send some farmhands out to herd these steers back. Though if you elf boys wanna waste your time driving our herd back then go right ahead.' He pointed. 'Follow the river east till you see a gorge on the right, beyond that's our ranch. Wouldn't advise riding too close, Mrs Gatlan don't take kindly to strangers and she's a crack shot with a rifle.'

'You elves haven't heard the last o' this!' shouted Whip. 'Pretty clever rustlin' up a storm like that but that hole in my wagon ain't gonna let me forget 'bout this too quickly.'

'Yeah, watch yer back, wizard man. Might have to face a little thunder yourself one day soon!' yelled Buck.

CHAPTER FOUR

★

Dugtown

I'd spent the night at Gung-Choux Village in Uncle Crazy Wolf's tepee. I hadn't planned to, but we'd stayed with the cattle for ages until the Gatlans had finally dispatched a few cowboys to round them up and drive them home, by which time it was nearly dark.

The next morning I decided I should make tracks back to Phoenix Rise, picking up some supplies on the way. My uncle cooked breakfast: fried bread and delicious honey. Then he announced, to my disbelief, that Chief Red Feather wanted to see me before I left.

'*Me*?' I swallowed hard. I had exchanged no more than one or two greetings with the chief during my visits over the years and even then I'd been terrified. He was such an important figure that I hardly dared look at him. 'But what does he want me for?'

'He wouldn't say, just said he wanted to see you in his tepee.'

I finished my breakfast then nervously climbed the stepped mound to the chief's tepee. The biggest dwelling in the village, it was beautifully decorated around the top with colourful spots and shapes, and in the centre with painted horses chasing each other, galloping and jumping. Taking a deep breath, I ducked to enter the flap-type door.

Lifting my head inside, I was met immediately by the village leader. An imposing figure, he wore a horned, plumed headdress, eagle feathers fanning out in an oval shape around his kind face. He led me inside to sit opposite him on a little wooden stool.

'These are dark days for the whole of the West Rock,' the chief began. 'I pray that the Great Spirit will soon bring your grandma home off the stricken arm.'

'Thank you, Chief Red Feather. I'm not giving up on her.'

'There is a pow wow – a meeting of all the elders – soon to discuss the unrest among the elf folk with regard to the human settlers. However, I fear I already know what the outcome will be – battle. The pale-skin settlers place heavy demands upon us. But it is not only the pale-skins; a troll railroad boss only recently tried to force through plans for a new rail service to Blackwater which will cut through the Chokewoods and some prime elf farmland.'

'The Chokewoods?!' I gasped. My uncle had told me how important these woods were to the elf folk for hunting. 'But a noisy steam train careering through the woods would scare off the deer and other animals.'

Nodding, the chief breathed a long sigh. 'Some of my braves say it is good that this has happened.

They say it is important to sharpen our fighting skills in battle otherwise we may lose them and become useless at defending ourselves. What do you say, Will?'

'I say talking is better than fighting, but I am not foolish, and I realise that there comes a time when you must fight.'

He nodded again slowly then went on. 'And who will you fight for, Will?'

'I am an elf, I will fight with the elf folk.'

'But you are a sky cowboy too. Half human. Does your heart lie fully with us? If I were to name you right now, do you know what I would call you?'

I shook my head.

'I would name you Two Hats. There are times while you are here in the village that I have seen you wear your uncle's feather headdress. But when you leave you remove it to put on your cowboy hat.'

'Yes, but I always keep a feather in it because I am proud of my elvish roots.' I glanced down to where I held my hat. Two Hats? My heart sank a little at the name. Once, when my uncle and I had discussed what my elf brave name should be, I'd come up with names like Spitting Snake, Growling Bear, Soaring Eagle, all of which were much better than Two Hats. 'I guess Two Hats would be better than being called Half-Breed.'

'A cruel taunt, but you must not look at it like that. You are as the Great Spirit would have you and I believe you to be a very special young man; one whose path on this rock is to be full of purpose. I believe you have come among us through your uncle at this time for a reason.'

'What do you mean?'

'Troubled waters lie ahead for my people, Will. There are rumours of an uprising among the sky cowboys, that they are gathering arms, organising into groups – armies. This is dangerous for they may take matters into their own hands. I fear that if we do not act soon, history will repeat itself and we will be driven from our homes.'

I told him about the guns I'd seen in the Gatlans' wagon and he nodded gravely.

'Perhaps more ominous is that the sky cavalry still do not show their faces. They hide their cards like the shrewdest of snake-poker players. Even the most cunning rune snake would be hard pressed to probe the mind of the high sheriff at this time. We must be mindful that the sky cavalry too are human, and if they support the ranchers then we really have trouble.'

'I am willing to do what I can to help.'

'I know you are, and that's why I summoned you. When you return to your ranch, keep an ear to the ground for anything that might suggest these rumours are true and the ranchers are planning to rise against us. You are the only one I can trust to walk among the humans and help us in this way.'

'I will, Chief Red Feather,' I said. 'You are my people, my family. I don't want to see any of you treated unfairly.'

Before I left the chief said, 'You would make a fine brave, Will. Has your uncle mentioned it?'

'Yes.'

'We could use you mightily, especially now that the

days grow darker for my people, but, of course, it is your decision.'

'I'd be honoured. I have spoken often about it to my uncle.'

'It is a short ceremony during which you will receive a new name – an elf name. You can continue with your apprenticeship to become a mage one day.'

Hopefully if I did become initiated, the chief would come up with a better name than Two Hats.

'It's not good the way things have been going of late,' I commented to Moonshine as we rode back to the settled lands, leaving Gung-Choux Village behind us.

'I know, Will. I miss Phoenix Creek,' she replied. 'I can't get used to living over this side of the rock.'

'You will, Shy, s'just gonna take time for both of us to adapt to things. Be better if Yenene moved into Phoenix Rise, though, might seem more normal then. It don't seem like home without her.'

'I'm still angry with those Gatlans. I gave the black stallions they were riding dagger eyes but they just glared back at me, snarling, like I was some dumb horse they could frighten with a scowl.'

I guessed what was coming next and mouthed the words as she spoke them.

'If only they knew my pa was in the sky cavalry, and that you and I have taken on snake-bellied trolls in Deadrock, then they wouldn't have been so cocky.'

We rode on.

'What did the chief say?' Moonshine asked after a while.

'He told me there's a big pow wow soon – that's a meeting with all the elders – to discuss the conflict with the new settlers.'

'What do you think's gonna happen?'

I didn't like worrying Moonshine but I never kept secrets from her. Shy was pretty resilient and we'd been through a lot together.

'Chief reckons the elves need to take a stand, show the settlers they're not just gonna sit back and be walked over; settlers treating them like they don't have rights, when elves have been living here for hundreds of years.'

'Yeah, and I figure those storm horses the Gatlans were riding think they're better than windhorses on account o' them being bigger. I might never make a good cart horse but without any wings there's no way those two'll be following me into the clouds. Say, where we going?'

'Gotta ride into Dugtown for supplies for the ranch.'

Dugtown was a town in a hurry. Once its site had been chosen by the settlers, building work had begun quickly. And the quickest and cheapest way to build a town – someone had suggested – was to dig it out of the ground. Almost all the buildings in Dugtown were 'pit houses'. A pit house, as the name suggests, is made by digging into the flat earth then building a roof over the top, using branches and sod. Some of the buildings had man-height wooden entrances with doors which opened onto a staircase descending into the ground.

It was a weird sort of a place, totally different to Oretown with its tall wooden buildings that closed in on the narrow streets. In Dugtown, all the store signs were at your feet: the Trunk and Arms saloon, the hotel, the sheriff's office, the bank, the jailhouse (I once got a crick in my neck staring down to read all the names as I passed). The tallest things in Dugtown, apart from the hotel and a couple of other one-storey buildings, were the long thin chimneys that poked out of the rooftops into the sky.

The sheriff, a blue-eyed, sandy-haired string bean of a man wearing a large silver star, stood in the entrance of the sheriff's office puffing on a bacca weed pipe. He hadn't taken his eyes off me since I'd arrived and now he called me over.

'Hey, boy. Come 'ere!'

'Me?'

'Don't see any other boys around.'

I rode Moonshine over and dismounted.

'Wouldn't happen to have been with an elf called Crazy Wolf yesterday, now would ya?' the sheriff asked.

I nodded. 'Yessir.'

'I figured it was you by the description that was given me. Ain't too many face-painted elf kids wearing cowboy hats around these parts.'

'I don't understand.'

'Been a complaint against you, kid. You an' that band of elf bandits you were riding with near the Gatlan place.' He pointed his pipe at me. 'So what's this Crazy Wolf to you?'

'He's my uncle.'

'Buck Gatlan says you were tryin' to rustle his cattle, showed me your uncle's handiwork on the side of his wagon, reckons it's gonna cost him a fair whack gettin' it repaired.'

'We weren't rustling anything. And a patch of a few cut planks o' timber'll fix the wagon.'

'Buck told me your uncle did it with his bare hands, using some sort of hocus pocus fireball.'

'Thunderball.'

'Pardon me?'

'It's called a thunderball. It's more wind than fire. Course, he can conjure a fireball too.'

'Think you're pretty smart, don't ya, kid? Well, if I was you I'd be careful. Ranch folk like the Gatlans don't have much time for smart-mouthed elf kids.'

'Half elf,' I corrected.

Staring at my hat, his mouth twitched and he puffed bacca weed smoke in my face.

'What's the idea with the hat, you some sorta elf rancher?'

'I work over at Phoenix Rise.'

'Tyrone's ranch? I know it well. Few good boys over there. Hope you ain't gonna make trouble for ol' Tyrone.'

'Ain't Tyrone's ranch. I'm Will Gallows, and the ranch belongs to my grandmother, though it belonged to my father, Dan Gallows, the former deputy sheriff of Oretown before her.'

'A deputy's boy should know better than to go around stirring up trouble.'

'The Gatlans were causing the trouble,' I said hotly. 'You haven't asked why my uncle blew a hole in their wagon. Maybe you should be over in Gung Village taking a look at the corn fields the Gatlans' cattle just trampled into the ground.'

He grunted dismissively. 'Just be thankful the Gatlans ain't pressin' charges.'

At that moment a drunken cowboy rolled out of the Trunk and Arms saloon. He called, 'Hey, Sheriff, you ain't lookin' for a deputy, are you?'

'No, an' if I was, a critter like you'd be the last person I'd employ.'

The man staggered up to us. 'Aw, how's a cowboy meant to feed himself when there ain't no work on this stupid side of the rock?'

'Only thing you been feeding yourself is Boggart's Breath whiskey. Maybe if you could see straight, you'd see your way to findin' a job.'

'Phooey. I'm tired o' lookin'. Ranches are so small, they don't need more than a couple o' hands to work the steers.'

'I'm pretty sure the Gatlan brothers are hirin' help, why don't you ride out there?'

'I'm 'bliged to you, Sheriff,' said the drunk. He tipped his hat then teetered and fell headlong into a brim-full water trough.

The sheriff sighed. 'C'mon, help me fish this good-for-nothing out o' here an' you can be on your way. Keep away from trouble an' that'll be the end o' the matter.'

I couldn't believe how the sheriff was twisting it so that I felt like it was my fault. After I'd finished helping him fish the out-of-work cowboy from the trough I led Shy over to the mercantile store and got the stuff I needed for the ranch. Then, still disgruntled at the way the sheriff had acted, I mounted Moonshine and left Dugtown behind me, heading for the open plains, and Phoenix Rise.

As we rode, Moonshine commented, 'Remind me never to drink from that trough again.'

CHAPTER FIVE

★

Phoenix Rise

The sun was high in the sky as I rode into Phoenix Rise. I hadn't planned to be away two days as I didn't like to neglect my chores. Though with the new ranch being a lot smaller I knew I could catch up pretty quickly. Tyrone, the ranch foreman the sheriff had mentioned, and the other sky cowboys could easily handle things while I was away.

I noticed that someone had fixed the wooden sign above the arched entrance to the ranch. It read:

WELCOME TO
PHOENIX RISE

I rode to the paddock then dismounted.

'See you later, Shy.' I gave her a pat on the neck. 'Tomorrow is back to business as usual. I'm sure you're tired. Been a long couple o' days and you've done a lot of flying about the rock.'

'I'm OK. I miss Jez, though. When we gonna see her again?' Moonshine asked.

'Soon, I hope. She'll probably come with us to Grandma's in a few days. Got to keep trying to persuade her to leave – and feeding her.'

All the ranch hands were agreed that while business was going well enough, the place was far too quiet without Yenene busily shuffling around giving orders, grumbling, laughing, helping, riding, roping. There was nothing she couldn't do or didn't know about ranching and we all missed her.

I wandered over to look at how the new barn was coming along when a voice behind me said, 'First thing Yenene'll say is that the barn's too small.'

I turned round to see Tyrone.

'I don't know if she will, Tyrone,' I said forlornly. 'She seems pretty determined to stay put.'

'Still ain't budgin', huh?' Sighing, he clapped a

big hand on my shoulder. 'I don't get it, she was so involved in organising the move over here then, when it's all finished, she won't come. She must've known all along she wouldn't be moving with us.'

'Reckon she did. I don't think any of us will ever understand cos none of us can get inside her head to see what's going on in there.'

'The place ain't the same without her – everyone says so; the other ranch hands are all just moping around, going through the motions. S'like the heart o' the place ain't here any more.'

'I'm not giving up, Tyrone, though it bothers me leaving my chores for the day to go flying off around the rock . . .'

Tyrone frowned. 'Don't wanna hear you talkin' like that again. Go for a week if you want, we know you're the last person to shirk your chores. You work as hard as the rest of us, and bringin' back your grandma would be the best thing that could happen to this here ranch.'

He turned to leave, then stopped.

'Oh, Will. I nearly forgot. There's a baby thunder dragon lying injured over by the creek. Looks like it's been shot. It won't let any of us near it. Maybe you

77

could go take a look, see if you can do that elf animal-talk thing.'

'Where exactly is it?'

'Not far from that clump of saddlewood trees.'

'I'll ride over there now.'

'OK. By the way, nice face paint. Suits you.'

I returned to the paddock and got Moonshine. She grumbled a bit as she'd been having a snooze. But when she heard about the thunder dragon she whinnied loudly.

'A thunder dragon, are you serious? Last time I got close to one o' those it singed my tail so bad I had to walk around funny for weeks trying to hide it between my legs.'

'Quit worrying, Shy, it's only a baby.'

'They're the worst. It was a young 'un did that to my tail.'

I won her over with the promise of a morning off the next day, and we flew across to the creek and found the dragon lying on the ground looking very distressed.

Its head and body were about the length of a steer, and its long spiny tail was as long again, making the young dragon quite an impressive-looking creature for a baby. I noticed it had small horns so it was a female.

Green and scaly, her body rippled with muscles and her wings and feet bore spear-sharp talons that could tear open the flesh of her prey; prey that included pick-toothed wolves, wasteland hyenas and fire-spitting eagles.

'That's a baby?' Moonshine baulked.

'Hey, friend, looks like you flew a little too close to the rock.'

As I stepped closer, the thunder dragon let out a high-pitched – *kweeeek*, swishing her tail. When she was fully grown, that sound would boom like the loudest bolt of thunder, making the earth tremble. Then she spewed out a jet of fire that stopped just short of scorching my knees. My heart raced as I realised that this creature, no bigger than a steer, could cook me in seconds.

'Whoah there, I mean you no harm. I'm a friend, an elf, I can understand you, if you'll speak to me. Tell me, who did this to you?'

The dragon fixed a sky-blue eye on me but held her tongue. Even though hunting thunder dragons was prohibited by order of the high sheriff, the creatures were wary of Rock folk. Understandably too. My pa told me that the poor things had been hunted to near extinction by the ancient settlers of the rock. The dragons had at one time been native to the West Rock, soaring freely over the rock tops and ridges, nesting, raising young without hindrance. Then came the first pioneers, ascending the rocky wilderness from the West Woods and Wastelands to lay claim to the mysterious new land with its dangers and bounty. Timid creatures, the dragons put up hardly any fight – even though bullets are unable to penetrate the skin of an adult – and when their eggs and young were stolen many moved on to parts of the West Woods and remote Wastelands where they could be left in peace.

'My name is Will, what do they call you?'

Again, the dragon was silent.

'OK, one thing I know is that thunder dragons aren't stupid, so I'm pretty sure you can understand me. And unless we stop that blood oozing out of you like snakes from a snake-bellied troll's guts you won't be breathing air, let alone fire.'

The dragon's expression softened, her ears had been flat to her neck, like Moonshine's when she senses danger, but now they began to prick forward slightly. Maybe I was beginning to get through.

I wished I had Uncle Crazy Wolf's magic book; I'd read a whole chapter on healing quite recently, though I could only remember bits and pieces. There had been too much to take in. No wonder so few apprentices ever made it through the rigorous training to become a medicine mage. Many try but few succeed, my uncle was always telling me, and nor should they. Bloodline is important, yes, but a true medicine mage will find his own way through the learning. A chief is chosen from among the tribe folk but a medicine mage is ordained by the spirits; in essence it is the spirits who choose who will carry the burden of the role.

Still, I did have some magic healing herbs in the pouch of Moonshine's saddle and I fetched them.

Then, removing my bandanna from around my neck, I held it out for the dragon to see.

'Best I can do is a good old-fashioned field dressing with some healing herbs but it should stem the flow, if you'll let me do it.'

And then the dragon wailed softly. She hadn't spoken but I sensed she was telling me it was OK. Slowly I moved closer to kneel beside her injured wing. If I'd misread the signal, I'd be flame-grilled in an instant, or feel dagger-sharp teeth close in round my head. But no, she let me move nearer. Using the magic herbs, I gently bound the wounded wing, blotting out the danger while I concentrated on tying a good knot that wouldn't loosen when the dragon moved her wing. She gave a shrill wince as I tightened it but allowed me to finish with nothing more than a few puffs of smoke from her flared nostrils. It was then I noticed the other wounds on the dragon's belly and my heart sank. She'd taken a peppering of bullets, probably from a Wynchester prairie rifle. This confirmed my fears as to why she had come down; the wing injury was bad but not bad enough to pull the dragon out of the sky. She had multiple wounds.

Carefully I sprinkled more of the healing herbs onto the wounds, the way Uncle Crazy Wolf had taught me. I focused my mind, my outstretched palms hovering over the injuries then I began to chant some magic words in the ancient elf language, at least the ones I could remember.

'Go,' she said suddenly, her voice soft.

'Your side, there are many wounds. I want to help.'

'Now!' she said firmly. I felt slightly bitter at the dragon's lack of gratitude and I started to tell her that, but my words were drowned out suddenly by an ear-splitting boom, like thunder. The ground trembled under my knees, and a dark shadow blotted out the sun, growing bigger and bigger.

An adult thunder dragon was plunging towards me.

My pa had told me that they only make that thunderous roar when they are angry and, as thunder dragons are timid beasts, it is rarely heard. It was certainly the first time I'd heard it and I was sure I'd never forget it.

As the dragon dived closer I saw its front claws, like giant stalactites, fixed to the middle of horizon-wide wings. Two huge black horns snaked out of the back of its head – it was a male.

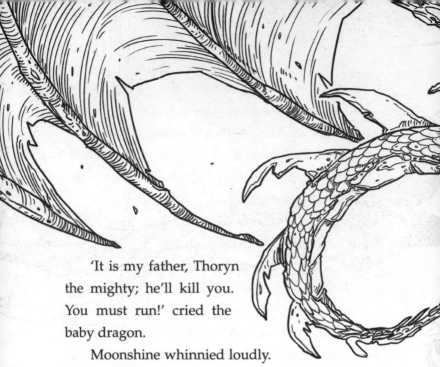

'It is my father, Thoryn
the mighty; he'll kill you.
You must run!' cried the
baby dragon.

Moonshine whinnied loudly.
'C'mon, Will. C'mon, I'm gonna need a head start to out
fly something as big as that.'

The young dragon emitted a squeal that her father
answered with another deafening roar.

My blood ran ice-cold. Heart galloping, I bolted
towards Shy who kneeled down to let me jump into the
saddle.

Dust from the dragon's powerful wing beats
engulfed us as Moonshine took to a gallop, spreading
her own wings which looked tiny compared to those

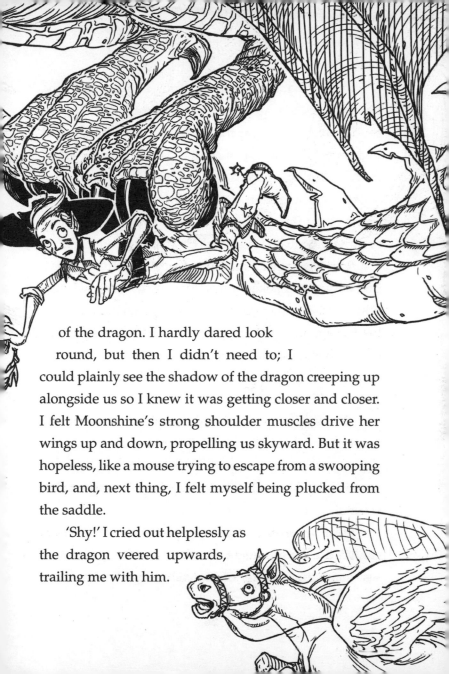

of the dragon. I hardly dared look
round, but then I didn't need to; I
could plainly see the shadow of the dragon creeping up
alongside us so I knew it was getting closer and closer.
I felt Moonshine's strong shoulder muscles drive her
wings up and down, propelling us skyward. But it was
hopeless, like a mouse trying to escape from a swooping
bird, and, next thing, I felt myself being plucked from
the saddle.

'Shy!' I cried out helplessly as
the dragon veered upwards,
trailing me with him.

I glanced at his green skin and yellow underbelly; his horned head was bigger than Moonshine and a dark, beady eye glowered at me. His teeth were the stuff of nightmares, the worst of which were the lower fangs that protruded up past his nostrils like a Deadrock stalagmite rising from the cave floor.

As the ground got further away I struggled to think of something to do, conscious I had only seconds to live. Thunder dragons are intelligent creatures, this one had probably only plucked me off to spare Moonshine's life, which was touching, but still wouldn't stop the dragon tossing me up in the air and into a shower of flames at any moment. Down below I heard the faint cries of the young dragon. Her father would finish me off quickly so he could tend to her.

'She needs you,' I cried. 'I didn't harm her, I swear I didn't harm her.' I watched as his dark eye jerked between me and the ground below. I swallowed a boulder-sized lump in my throat – I was completely at the mercy of this giant of the sky.

Still the wounded young one called from where she lay on the ground. Out of the corner of my eye I was sure I caught sight of Moonshine, probably feeling pretty powerless too.

And suddenly I was falling. Amazingly, the dragon had let me go. Not tossed me into an inferno. Why? Was he hoping I'd dash my bones on the rocky ground below? For a few pounding heartbeats all I could hear was the rush of air past my ears then the wonderful sound of a horse's neigh.

Moonshine swooped beneath me and I landed belly down, facing her rump, as her tail swished and tickled my nose. She flexed her wings, fencing me in and slowing down, allowing me time to scrabble round till I was facing the right way. I pushed myself up into the saddle then took the reins.

'You OK?' she asked, streaking off in full flight.

'A bit shook up. Thank goodness for critter chatter, that's all I can say.'

'I was sure you were a gonner that time; I can't believe it dropped you.'

'He didn't drop me. He let me go.'

'Let you go, but why?'

'Dunno. I told him I didn't harm his young 'un – guess he must've believed me. But I still think we should get outta here in case he changes his mind.'

'You try to do someone a favour, eh?' Moonshine grumbled, referring to my field-dressing attempt.

'Sure feel sorry for that little dragon, though. I hope she makes it through.'

Back at the ranch, as I was leading Moonshine to the paddock, I bumped into Tyrone.

'Well, you ain't lookin' too scorched so I reckon you must've fixed up that poor dragon.'

'I would have if her pa hadn't turned up.'

'What! So that's what I heard. You OK? I was in the barn when I heard a roar like thunder only different.'

'That was her pa, mad-looking critter, though he didn't harm me. Who would've shot the young dragon, though? Her belly was badly peppered.'

'None of our boys, y'can be sure.'

'How far west does the Gatlan ranch extend? Sure feels like their handiwork.'

'I heard they bought out Luke Handold's place, he owned a few acres east of our own boundary. Rumour is they may have used a little persuasion, if you catch my drift.'

'But if they bought Handold's place then that makes them our . . . neighbours!'

'S'right.'

'Well, I bet it was one o' them shot it, or maybe even Buck's wife. Yesterday I heard Whip say she's pretty trigger happy with a rifle.'

'I know you wanna turn in, Will, but I gotta show you something.' Tyrone handed me a leaflet. 'The Gatlans dropped it by this morning.'

RANCHERS' MEETING
Tomorrow night
in Trunk & Arms Saloon, Dugtown.
Angry at new land allotments?
Mad at the high sheriff's
refusal to listen to our gripes?
It's time to take action.

'Are you going, Tyrone?'

'Yeah, but only to see what all the hullabaloo's about. And to see what those dolt-head Gatlan boys are up to. You can be sure they ain't got everybody's interest at heart.'

'I had a run in with them,' I told Tyrone, 'when I was visiting my uncle. They let their cattle roam all over Crazy Wolf's corn fields. We drove them off then the Gatlans showed up, madder than a couple o' skinned clattersnakes. Shouting the odds they were till Crazy Wolf conjured a thunderball and cast it into the side of their wagon. Blew a hole big as a watermelon, it did.'

'In that case might be best if you stayed away from the meeting.'

I nodded. 'I plan to. Sherriff of Dugtown's already got an eye on me on account of the Gatlans putting in a complaint.' But part of me, like Tyrone, did want to find out what all the hullabaloo was about. Especially if, as I thought, it concerned my people (on my elf side, of course). Wasn't this the sort of thing Chief Red Feather wanted me to keep an ear to the ground for? Tyrone would be there but I couldn't expect him to remember it all. No, I had to figure out a way of being at the meeting but not being at the meeting.

I went to my room and crawled into my bed, exhausted. I fell asleep thinking about Grandma and hoping she would have a quake-free night over on the stricken western arm.

CHAPTER SIX

★

The Trunk and Arms Saloon

'I'm tying y'up outside the hotel here, Shy, on account of the Gatlans might recognise you, and cos it seems like half the horses on West Rock are tied up by the Trunk and Arms saloon,' I said.

It was the night of the meeting and we'd ridden into Dugtown, stopping outside the Hotel.

'Aw, but I saw the Gatlans' two black mares. Why don't you tie me beside them so I can tell them what I think of them and their lousy owners?'

I gave Moonshine a pat on the neck. 'Easy, girl, they're not worth getting all heated up about. They haven't had the good breeding you have. Now, stay put, I'm gonna see if I can sneak round the back of the saloon. See ya soon.'

I walked down between the sheriff's office and the gunsmith's wishing all the constructions were as big as the hotel. It's very hard to look inconspicuous when you're twice as tall as the buildings.

At the end of the alley I cut left along the back of the sheriff's office then past the empty crates and barrels of the mercantile store until I smelled the stench of Boggart's Breath whiskey and bacca-weed smoke pouring out of windows and chimney-like air vents that protruded from the saloon roof. More wooden crates filled with brown glass bottles and smelly trash cans lay strewn along the back of the saloon. The whole place stank, and I couldn't understand why so many sky cowboys would spend so much time in there.

Crawling on my belly up to the ground-level window I peered inside. Bacca-weed smoke hung thick in the air, glowing purple in the saddlewood lamp light. A long wooden bar, fronted by bar stools, ran the full length of the saloon. Perched on the stools and seated on chairs placed around small saloon tables were ranchers and sky cowboys. Some played snake poker but most just

92

sat drinking Boggart's Breath and talking loudly over the music of a tinkling piano. Tyrone sat in the corner and I thought he looked awkward, he wasn't one for sitting in saloons and I'd never known him to drink Boggart's Breath. Then I heard another noise; someone was trying to call order by clanging a spoon on the side of a beer glass. Glancing round to see who it was I caught sight of the Gatlan brothers for the first time.

'Been a long day, gentlemen,' Buck boomed. 'So I'll get to the point o' why my brother Whip and me called this here meeting. We wanted to ascertain if there's any cowboys out there feel that we settlers been unfairly treated since movin' from Oretown and the western arm. Dunno 'bout you boys but I ain't used to having just a little bit of land to range my cattle and I ain't used to livin' with hostile neighbours. Why, only two days ago we were attacked by elf folk. Tell 'em what happened, Whip.'

The place erupted in jeers until Whip strode forward raising his hand for order.

'We were travellin' by cart into Dugtown when we caught a bunch of elves tryin' to rustle our cattle from under our very noses.'

My jaw dropped open as I listened to the same dirty, rotten lie they'd told the sheriff. But worse was to come.

'More than twenty of 'em, there was, right nasty bunch too, carryin' rifles and spears.'

I couldn't believe my ears; there'd been seven of us and not one of us had carried a rifle: guns and rifles ain't the elf way of things. Elves are more at home with bow and arrows, blowgun or spear, and then only for hunting. Elves are a peaceful race but that doesn't mean they'll be trodden on, either.

'Course we stood up to them,' Whip went on. 'We drove our cart over and told them we'd get the sheriff onto them, but they just laughed right in our faces. Then one of them starts yellin' a whole lot of mumbo jumbo, starts that hocus-pocus thing you probably heard some elves can do. Well, let me tell you, I never heard or saw anything like this before. The crazy wizard elf conjured bullets the size o' watermelons with his bare hands, out o' thin air, swirlin' and makin' a noise like thunder, they shot up our cart to smithereens.'

Whip was a better storyteller than Miss Wyatt, my old teacher at Oretown elementary.

'Don't know what the big fuss is about,' Tyrone

piped up from the corner of the saloon. 'Ain't hardly seen any elf folk since movin' out here. Figure they're the type that keeps themselves to themselves.'

'I've seen elf kids sneakin' round my farm, with a mind on stealin' my chickens,' said a skinny rancher.

'Reckon it was elves stole a coupla my steers only last week,' piped up another.

Buck looked at Tyrone. 'You figured wrong, mister. The elves are just foolin' you into thinkin' that. I know for a fact they ain't happy 'bout us bein' on their land, and first time our backs are turned, they're plannin' on doin' somethin' 'bout it.'

A cowboy shouted, 'So what are you saying? That the elves are planning some sort of offensive.'

'I'm sure of it. I've heard stuff, rumours that even now they're plotting to murder us, our wives and children in our very beds. The magic man said he can turn invisible, sneak into our houses while we're asleep!'

The saloon erupted in jeers.

'They ain't normal!'

'Murderin' scum.'

'I heard they eat their own children, boil them in big pots on the fire.'

Buck was beginning to enjoy himself. He had the whole saloon eating out of his hands. I liked the sound of the invisibility idea but was pretty sure it wasn't in any of Uncle Crazy Wolf's leather-bound volumes of magic.

'We gotta do something.'

'Yeah, if this is true then we can't just sit back and wait for it to happen.'

A grin cut Buck's face in two. His evil plan, his lies, were being sucked up by the ranchers like an anteater slurping up a mouthful of termites. He had them exactly where he wanted them.

'What do we do?'

Buck took a swig of beer, wiping his mouth with his sleeve. 'I say we take the 'nitiative. I say . . . we strike first!'

'What about the sky cavalry?'

'Sittin' on their lazy butts in Mid-Rock City. They don't want to do too much unless it affects them directly. And this doesn't affect them directly. They're sittin' up there in Fort Mordecai in their fancy uniforms, eatin' good food, in good jobs, while those of us down here lucky enough to have a job are strugglin' to make ends meet. We've got a town to make, ranches to build and the elves won't even let us cut timber.'

'But we ain't soldiers, Buck, an' there's hundreds o' them elf critters.'

'I say we can beat them if we gather us together enough good men. I know I mentioned they had some metal but most o' them only got bows and arrows. We'll be armed with rifles and guns, my brother an' I will see to that.'

I noticed his voice gathering urgency, as the ranchers nodded to each other, murmuring.

'And we got windhorses too. We can sweep down on them just like the sky cavalry – better than the sky cavalry.'

'You're forgetting 'bout the medicine mage!' a familiar, muffled-sounding female voice spoke up from the back of the saloon.

The whole place went quiet. You could've heard a pin drop.

Squinting through the bacca-weed smoke I could just make out a wide-brimmed black hat that sent an ice-cold shudder down my spine, even before I saw the dark staring eyes and the dirty bandages.

It was the wolfer who'd tried to rustle our horses at Phoenix Creek.

The fact that no one was sitting near her doubly made up my mind it was her, as she stank so bad. But what was she doing at the meeting?

After a pause, she went on, 'Who's to say he won't conjure up his magic against us, shoot our horses out of the sky with those watermelon bullets you told us about?'

Buck's face reddened. He clenched his fists. 'Freedom never came without a price, y'know. But maybe you're happy to play second fiddle to a bunch of green, long-eared farmers. Maybe you don't mind letting them squeeze you into a tiny corner of the Rock, where there's no room to breathe, let alone range cattle.'

'Ain't saying that, I'm saying there are a few more things I reckon need addressin', and the main ones are that we get the sky cavalry on our side. We don't stand a chance without them. And we run the risk of them coming down on the elf side of things, if we don't factor them in somehow. The second thing is that we need to get rid of the elf medicine mage. He's the real threat.'

My jaw dropped. I was horrified at how cold and

calculated her words sounded. It was also chilling to hear her refer to him as the medicine mage and not just the hocus-pocus man.

She went on, 'The mage is a powerful tribesman, not only in a magical sense but he is of great spiritual importance, like a sort of talisman. I got no love for elf folk but I know a thing or two about this person, only the chief is more powerful.'

Buck's eyes narrowed. 'How do you know all this? And don't mind me saying, but how come you're so interested in gettin' involved? You sure don't look like a rancher to me.'

'I'm a wolfer by trade,' she explained. 'And I know all this cos I lived among the elf folk a long time ago till we had a fallin' out. Now I hate them all, but especially the medicine mage – call it a personal vendetta, if you like.'

'Personal vendetta,' Buck echoed stroking his chin. 'Go on.'

She took a swig of her drink. 'The elves believe if the mage is with them then any battle is already won, meaning that if something were to happen to him either during battle or before it . . .'

Buck grinned. 'Then the heart would be knocked out of the whole tribe.'

'Precisely. It would make defeating them a whole lot easier, in spite of their greater numbers.'

Buck nodded. 'Reckon I'm startin' to get interested, lady. What did you say your name was?'

'Hyde. Imelda Hyde. Be willin' to share with you an idea that might just kill both birds with the one stone.' She cackled like an old witch and Buck raised an eyebrow.

'Let's hear it.'

She drained her beer glass, wiping her mouth with her sleeve. 'Ain't for the whole saloon's ears, if you'll pardon me. No offence to the good folk of the saloon here. Though I'd be willin' to speak with you gentlemen afterwards. In private.'

I was suddenly aware of hurried footsteps behind me but before I could turn round, a heavy boot came down hard on the back of my neck pinning me to the ground.

'Well now, I knew I saw someone noseyin' in the window. Looks like I found me an elf spy.'

My stomach churned and I felt my heart pound

against the dirt. It was a Gatlan voice and it had to be Whip because I was still staring at Buck through the window.

Grabbing me by the ankles, Whip shoved me through the open window into the saloon.

I cried out, arms flailing as I tumbled down onto the bar top. Glasses scattered, smashing onto the floor, and I found myself staring up into the hairy nostrils of a whip-tailed goblin. The goblin rose to his feet.

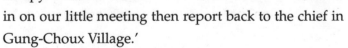

'You spilled my drink, stupid kid,' he rasped.

Buck grabbed me by the shirt collar and pulled me off the bar. 'Well, look at this, everybody,' he boomed. 'A half-breed elf spy. Come to listen in on our little meeting then report back to the chief in Gung-Choux Village.'

Whip entered the saloon doors. 'This kid was with the wizard tryin' to rustle our cattle. They've sent him to spy on us, find out where we live so the hocus-pocus man can come in and slit our throats.' Whip ran a hand over his neck.

Anger welled up inside me until I couldn't contain it and I blurted out, 'Don't listen to them. They're telling a pack of lies. It was the Gatlans' cattle that were trampling all over elf corn fields!'

But the ranchers clustered around me, forming a circle, and began pushing me back and forth to one another yelling insults. Some of them spat in my face.

'Wizard spy!'

'Thief!'

'Murderer!'

I felt dizzy and sick; tears welled up in my eyes, blurring the angry faces as they hurled more and more insults at me.

Then suddenly a gunshot rang out.

Tyrone had fired a round from his six-shot into the roof.

'Enough,' he shouted. 'The boy's done nothing. Look at you, like a pack of animals bayin' for blood. Why, you oughta be ashamed of yourselves.'

The pushing stopped and I staggered, like a newborn calf, in the midst of the widening circle.

'This scrawny good-for-nothin' something to you, cowboy?' Buck drawled.

'Yeah, he's somethin' to me – kid 'n' me work the same ranch.'

The angry faces gasped, gawking at me like I was an exhibit in the old Oretown museum.

'Rancher, y'say? Last time I saw him he was riding with a band of renegade elf braves, rustling cattle.'

'I tell you he's a sky cowboy.'

'Then it's time he started acting like one.' Buck glowered at me. 'If you ain't *for* us, kid, then you're against us, and if you're against us then one day you're gonna be dead meat. So if you're smart, you'll keep that big mouth o' yours shut.'

But Tyrone wasn't finished. 'Elf folk don't want trouble, Buck, but if you provoke them you might find you've bitten off more than you can chew. C'mon, Will, we're gettin' outta this rotten place.'

As we left, Buck called, 'You can tell your elf friends, especially that wizard man, to watch their backs. Time has come for elf folk to start acting civilised and give way when it's called for.'

I thought Buck and Whip were probably the least

civilised folk I'd ever met. I turned, wanting to shout something back, but Tyrone steered me round with a big arm.

'Leave it, Will. They ain't worth it. They've been itchin' for a quarrel with the elf natives since they moved out here.'

'I heard it all from the window. I reckon that right now they're probably the two most dangerous men on the whole of the West Rock. They're going to start a war.'

'They'll certainly take some watchin'. Goodness knows what kind of skulduggery they're plannin' next. You'll have to be careful, Will. Those two lowlifes will be gunnin' for you. Don't be ridin' near the boundary fences that border the Gatlan's ranch. They get you out in the open, you never know what they'll do.'

'Don't worry, Tyrone, I can look after myself. But I have to go to Gung-Choux Village tomorrow and warn Uncle Crazy Wolf.'

'Do you think it's safe ridin' over there?'

'Probably not but I gotta do it, though I don't like leaving you and the others again so soon. I promise I'll work night and day to catch up on my chores.'

'I told you I didn't want you talkin' like that. You do what you think is right. I just wish things were more normal round here for you, kid; that your grandma was here at the ranch, and that folk would try an' get along with one another.'

'I do too, Tyrone,' I replied, 'and I'm gonna figure a way through all this. But the way things are getting around here, Yenene is probably safer staying put on the western arm.'

I tipped my hat to Tyrone then headed for the hotel to fetch Shy. I had a lot to tell her on the ride home.

CHAPTER SEVEN
★
Drums of War

The next morning I packed a bag for the trip to Gung-
Choux Village. I'd decided to stay for a few days. I
felt strange, like I wanted to be away from Phoenix
Rise. I almost couldn't wait to leave.

I didn't tell Tyrone how I felt as he'd maybe read a
whole lot into it. It was probably just because of what
had happened with the Gatlans last night. I recalled the
scene in the saloon, the faces of the ranchers as they'd
pushed me around, the jeers, the taunts, the hatred. I
wanted no part of it. Most of them were human too, and
for the first time in my life I began to dislike the human
side of me. I got my human side from Pa but he was
different. He stood tall among all the other Oretown
folk, not just physically but morally too. He would've

known what to do about this situation. I just wished he was still around so I could ask him.

Soon Moonshine and I were riding a steady pace out of Phoenix Rise. My eyes raked the flat ranch land to the west of ours for any sign of the Gatlans but all was quiet. We followed the river into the valley and onwards until finally I caught sight of the big totem pole up ahead. Smoke signals rose into the air and, reading them, my heart sank: it was a call to war.

I'd been talking to Shy as we rode to help pass the time for both of us. Shy was the best horse a sky cowboy could ever have. She'd wanted to fly but I said there was no rush. It was hard to get a feel for the countryside from the air and I wanted to familiarise myself with the lie of the land from ground level.

The eastern arm still felt a bit new to me. It wasn't long till the subject of the Gatlans came round.

'You needn't worry about the sky cavalry,' Shy said. 'They'll do the right thing by the elf folk. They've always been on the side of justice.'

'Even so, Shy, I'd sure like to see them taking more of an interest in what's going on down here. I don't think they realise how serious things have got.'

'Maybe they don't know.'

'It's the responsibility of the sheriff of Dugtown to keep them informed.'

'Wouldn't be the first sheriff not to be doing his job.' Shy was referring to Sheriff Slugmarsh of Oretown who'd been as crooked as a barrel of fish hooks.

We rode on through the valley. Finally the conical tepees of Gung-Choux Village came into view.

And that was when I heard it.

Boom! Boom! Boom!

At first I thought it was thunder, or worse, a thunder dragon, but it was too rhythmical to be anything like that.

Shy whinnied nervously.

Then I knew exactly what it was.

'War drums,' I breathed.

'What?'

'It's OK, Shy, it's the beat of elven war drums. Looks like the pow wow meeting with the elders went the way Chief Red Feather said it would go.'

'What do you mean?'

'The beating of the war drum symbolises the mood of the clan. It means the elves have decided that soon there will be a call to arms for the coming battle.'

As we rode close to the village I noticed more signs that conflict was coming. Elf braves had been posted at intervals around the perimeter of the village. They were on foot, carrying spears, bows and arrows and mace. Their green faces were streaked with bold lines of red paint – war paint!'

One brave thrust a spear towards me as I approached but he soon lowered it, raising a hand in welcome as he recognised me.

The whole atmosphere in the village felt very different. I dismounted and led Shy through the colourful tepees, passing folk busying themselves. But I was aware that these were not the chores of normal day-to-day village life. Smiles were few, brows were furrowed. The two braves who had previously been making the canoe now sat binding turkey-feather fletching to the ends of arrows. The blacksmith who normally beat horseshoes now brought his hammer down on spear tips. Even children sat painting thunder dragons and pick-toothed wolves on round wooden shields, while their mothers repaired and strengthened the damaged ones.

At the foot of the totem pole, behind two large painted drums, stood the tallest, most muscle-bound elf I'd ever seen. His bare chest was covered in war paint and he had arms thick as tree trunks. In each hand he grasped enormous wooden drumsticks which, grunting loudly, he pounded into the drum skins, almost as though he were trying to split them both open.

Beside the drummer I caught sight of my uncle sitting cross-legged, both hands outstretched towards the sky. He wore a mage bonnet, a sunburst of white fire-spitting eagle plumes, with buffalo horns and a beaded brow band, and his face was painted in bold white stripes.

'What's he doing?' Shy asked.

'He's in a trance.'

'What's a trance?'

In my studies I'd just finished a chapter on spiritual trances so I knew all about this.

'The medicine mage is responsible for communicating with elf ancestors of the spirit world; usually in times of need, to ask for their advice,' I informed her. 'The ritual begins with the mage chanting, then his spirit leaves his body, ascending into the Upper World to meet with the spirits. It's a bit like a spiritual council meeting. This way the medicine mage is able to gather the support of spirits and forefathers for any venture. Normally it's nothing to do with conflict, although there have been a few tribal disputes over the years. It's more likely to be a discussion over the coming harvest, or maybe the weather or other domestic stuff. It's dangerous too. Failure to return from a trance can lead to death so we need to be careful not to disturb him.'

I knew the beating of the drum helped the mage to achieve his altered state of consciousness. Moving closer I saw that the drums had pictures, little pictographs of stick men running after deer and horses, and a rainbow-bridge, symbolising the bridge between

the three physical and spiritual worlds: the Upper, the Rock and the Lower Worlds.

Suddenly my uncle returned. He opened his eyes, blinked then stared straight ahead for a while. When he saw me he smiled, beckoning for me to come to him.

'Go get a drink and rest up, Shy. I'll see you later.'

Uncle Crazy Wolf put an arm on my shoulders. 'Back so soon, you are keen to learn. Have you read about trances?'

'Yes.'

'Good. One day you will come with me to walk between the worlds.'

My stomach fluttered with excitement. 'What's it like?'

'Powerful, soul stirring, humbling.' He smiled. 'And a hundred more words that will all be hopelessly inadequate at describing what it is like – but you will see.'

'Who did you meet with?'

'Great chiefs of the past, mages, elder clan women of standing from long-gone villages.'

'You mean there were elves there from the western arm villages, like the old clearing near Phoenix Creek?'

He nodded, a grave expression suddenly spreading across his face.

'All are agreed, we must take a stand if we are to prevent history repeating itself. We must not let the human settlers drive us from our land the way our forefathers were forced from the western arm by the early pioneers.'

He rose and we walked to his tepee.

'I have important news for both you and Chief Red Feather.' I began setting a pot of water on the fire to make some coffee. 'The chief instructed me to keep an ear to the ground for rumours of an uprising among the new ranchers.'

'I knew there must be a reason for such an early return, go on.'

'You remember the Gatlan brothers; you added a great big lookout hole to their wagon?'

'Don't think I'll forget those two ugly mugs in a hurry.'

'They're spreading lies about the elf folk, about you too. They're telling everyone, including the sheriff of Dugtown, that we were trying to rustle their cattle that day, and worse still that elf folk have been plotting to murder ranch folk and their families. They held a big meeting in a Dugtown saloon trying to rally support.'

'They get any?'

'Yes. It's getting more serious by the minute. An evil wolfer who calls herself Imelda Hyde reckons she has a plan that could get the support of the sky cavalry and at the same time get rid of you – she even mentioned a vendetta!'

'What did you say her name was?'

'Imelda Hyde. Why?'

'Hyde!' His eyes flashed with anger and fear. 'No. It couldn't be, could it?'

'Couldn't be what?'

'Many years ago, I had a young apprentice went by that name. A born medicine mage she was too – strong spirited and a quick learner. She showed much promise until she began meddling with the darker side of the magic when my back was turned. I warned her of the dangers the dark side could bring but she wouldn't listen, so I told her she could no longer be my apprentice. Later that day I recovered some dark magic books she'd taken from my tent library so she couldn't practice the magic any more.'

'What?!' I couldn't believe it, but it made sense. The moment when Yenene shot her hat off back at Phoenix

Creek and I'd glimpsed her pointed ears flashed through my mind. 'So that's how she knew so much about the medicine mage and how important they are to the tribe.'

'She would know a great deal.'

'Her face was covered in bandages. Do you know what happened to her?'

He nodded slowly. 'She went into a rage the night I told her I could no longer keep her as my apprentice; she tried to kill me by setting fire to my tepee. However, it didn't go as planned and, as well as the tepee, her own clothes caught fire. I hurried out unharmed and rushed to extinguish the flames with a windball but she was badly burned. I could've healed her over time with medicine magic but the other villagers banished her from the tribe after that so I couldn't help her.' Uncle Crazy Wolf sighed. 'What was her plan?'

'I don't know. She spoke to the Gatlans privately after the meeting but I don't like the look of her. You'll need to be on your guard.'

'This is solemn news indeed and news we must pass on to Chief Red Feather without delay. It involves what the chief fears most – if the sky cavalry become embroiled and take sides, rather than keeping the peace in all this, then it could spell disaster for us. Where was the sheriff of Dugtown when all this was going on?'

'Nowhere to be seen, not that it would have made any difference; I'm pretty sure the Gatlans got him eating outta their hands.'

'This is all as the spirits predicted. One spoke of a wolf crawling into our midst, and of a great darkness just before the conflict – could mean this Hyde woman. They advised we tread carefully, that the hostiles would be as wily as a fox, and their methods as winding as the trail of a clattersnake. Preparations for battle are underway, as you can see, though we do not intend to strike – merely to defend ourselves. And all this does not mean you can neglect your studies. They will help you in any forthcoming conflict. But one thing I must ask, Will, who will you fight for? You are of mixed loyalties – this fight is not yours.'

'I will fight for what is right,' I replied decisively. 'I will fight to defend the elf folk.'

'This is what I had hoped you would say. The elves will be truly honoured to have you on their side.'

'Now, will you come with me to Chief Red Feather's

tepee to tell him the news?' I asked.

He nodded gravely then, putting his arm round my shoulder, we started out through the village.

I spent the following days learning about elf magic, covering more than I'd learned in all the months I'd been visiting. We started with healing magic which is the very core of medicine magic. Then we went on to study spirit mediation or spirit chatter, as I called it – I even managed a short trance, but not long enough to enter into the Upper World to speak with the old elf ancestors of the tribe. Then I learned about rune-casting to predict the future, fireball conjuring, wraith binding, arrow bending and other stuff. Uncle Crazy Wolf was inspired; I'd never seen him so fired up to teach me magic before. Each night I collapsed into bed exhausted.

Inside the camp was busy, but outside was quiet – we never saw or heard a thing – certainly nothing hostile. The Gatlans were nowhere to be seen. Once I rode back to Phoenix Rise and even Tyrone said he'd seen neither hide nor hair of the Gatlans for days. What were they up to?

★ ★ ★

Then, one dark night a week later, the Gatlans played their ace.

And, like a striking rune snake during a snake-poker game, it was deadly.

A sound like a thunder dragon's roar woke me; six or more low booms. The noise was distant but definitely reverberating from somewhere on the eastern arm. It was like thunder dragons were all over the place on this side of the rock. I got up to look outside the tepee but could see nothing but stars. Had I been dreaming? I crawled back inside where Uncle Crazy Wolf still snored loudly in his bed.

I lay down and stared at the tapering roof of the tepee. Through the chimney hole it was pitch-black. And soon I went back to sleep.

The next morning, I woke at sunrise and got up. I'd forgotten all about the noises that had disturbed my sleep. I wanted to practise the arrow bending I'd been learning, before my uncle rose and we started something new. Carrying my bow and arrow to the old gnarled saddlewood tree on the edge of the village,

120

I shot arrows at the tree, trying to bend them with my mind as they tore through the air. At first I was hopeless and the arrow flew straight as a totem pole. I could hit the tree OK, that was the easy part, but I couldn't focus my mind enough to move the arrow in midair. Getting annoyed just made it worse so I took a break and sat under the tree for a while taking deep breaths. It was the best thing I could've done cos when I resumed, to my delight, I was able to bend the arrow in an ark shape through the sky to strike the centre of the tree. I punched the air, feeling very pleased with myself, but as I did so I spotted a group of mounted winged horses descending on the village. The horses' shiny tack glinted in the sunlight, as did the sabres their mounts carried – it was the sky cavalry. But why were the sky cavalry coming to Gung-Choux Village?

I was much too curious to continue with my training so, collecting my arrows from the trunk of the saddlewood tree, I replaced them in my quiver and hurried back into the village. I hadn't gone far when I was almost stampeded by the enormous elf drummer.

'The sky cavalry are here. They take your uncle!' he roared.

'What? Take him where?'

'They say they want to question him. The new fort was attacked during the night. There is much destruction; they blame Crazy Wolf's magic.'

I followed the elf drummer. The village was in turmoil, elf braves had gathered in groups holding spears, women wailed and little ones cried. I hadn't seen so many sky cavalry soldiers since I'd stayed at Fort Mordecai months earlier. There must have been at least twenty of them, on horseback, in full uniform, sabres by their sides. There could be no doubt this was a formal visit.

Three cavalrymen on foot led my uncle away, hands tied behind his back. They knew that the power of the medicine mage is in his hands and that it is vital to bind them. Other cavalrymen emerged from his tepee carrying boxes that they tipped onto the ground. Books and mage herbs fell out and the men kicked through them, like they were looking for something. Any elf braves who tried to stop them were quickly surrounded by sabre-wielding soldiers and brusquely pushed back.

The troops led Crazy Wolf over to the sheriff of Dugtown who looked at him disdainfully then nodded. 'That's him.'

'Will!' Crazy Wolf called, struggling to release the grip of the burly cavalrymen. 'Wait, I must speak with my nephew.'

I fought my way towards him. 'What's going on?'

'Someone attacked the new fort, killing the soldier guards,' gasped Crazy Wolf. 'They are saying I destroyed it with thunderballs.'

I remembered the noises during the night, the noises I'd thought were a thunder dragon.

'But that's ridiculous.' I turned to the sheriff and pleaded. 'My uncle was here all night, I was with him. You're making a terrible mistake.'

'You again?' he snarled. 'Thought I'd told you to keep out of trouble. This don't concern you, half-breed. Leave it to the sky cavalry.'

'But it's a set-up. Can't you see?'

'Save it for the trial, kid.'

'Don't worry, Uncle Crazy Wolf, I'll speak to the high sheriff, he'll listen to reason, if this idiot won't.'

I felt a mix of anger and fear. I remembered what Imelda Hyde, the old wolfer had said in the saloon. If something were to happen to the medicine mage then the heart would be knocked out of the whole tribe. Could this be the beginning of the great darkness the spirits had foretold?

One of the cavalrymen who held my uncle scowled at me. 'Step aside, kid, he's coming with us.'

'Where are you taking him?'

At first he didn't answer and I yelled again, 'Where are you taking him?'

'Mid-Rock City – crime this serious is outside the control of the local sheriff.'

Chief Red Feather appeared and shook his spear at the men who held Crazy Wolf. 'This is a great evil!' he cried. 'My elder mage has been nowhere near your fort, nor were any of my braves.'

The sheriff hissed, 'Ain't a weapon on the West Rock could pepper solid, six-foot thick wooden stockade with holes the size of watermelons. Got your wizard man's hocus pocus written all over it.'

'I smell the Gatlans in this!' I cried. 'And I'll prove it.'

'Like I said, save it for the trial,' said the sheriff.

They put my uncle onto the back of a cavalryman's horse and they rode off to jeers and cries from the elf braves.

I stared after them, hardly able to take in what had happened.

No sooner had they left than I began saddling Moonshine for the flight to Mid-Rock City.

'Will, what's happened? Where are they taking Uncle Crazy Wolf?' asked Moonshine.

'They've arrested him for murder, Shy. Looks like the sky cavalry aren't always on the side of justice.'

'I don't believe it.'

'I'm sure the Gatlans are behind this. They've set up Crazy Wolf.' I fastened the saddle buckle. 'We're riding out after him, Shy.'

A voice behind me said, 'Will.' It was one of the elders. 'The chief wants to see you on the mound.'

'OK,' I replied. 'Sit tight, Shy. We're flying to see the damage to the new fort, then on to Mid-Rock City right after I've spoken with the chief.'

I walked up the steps of the mound to the chief's tepee. Inside Chief Red Feather sat, his brow deeply furrowed.

I took off my hat and bowed. 'Chief Red Feather.'

'This is what I feared – now the sky cavalry show their hand, like gloating snake-poker players. But worse still, we have lost your uncle; our medicine mage and greatest asset in battle.'

'I'm going after him, Chief Red Feather. I'll speak with the high sheriff, Septimus Flynt, I fought alongside him in Deadrock Tin Mine. I'll make him see sense. He's a good man, and on the side of justice. He'll understand there's been a mistake.'

The chief put his hand on my shoulder and I felt a lump in my throat. I wasn't a brave, but my uncle had told me that it was considered an honour among braves for the chief to put his hand on you in this manner.

'You have much courage, young Will.' He paused. 'But you do not have to do this alone; I will send some braves with you.'

'Thank you, Chief, but it might be better if I travel by myself.' I held out my hat with its single feather sticking up from the crown. 'This hat will get me into Fort Mordecai but it is for this feather that I ride.'

He smiled. 'I understand. Then may the spirits ride with you. There is much at stake – without our medicine mage the battle is over before it has begun.'

'I will not fail. The Gatlans won't get away with this.'

'Spoken like a true brave. You have your uncle's spirit and wisdom.'

As we rode past the thunder-dragon totem pole, I noticed that the big elf now stood forlornly, his two arms by his side.

'Stop a minute, Shy,' I told her.

I leaped out of the saddle and sprang towards the elf. The drumstick clubs lay on top of the drums and I grabbed them. They were so heavy; I could only just lift them. Gritting my teeth I raised the club and began to beat the drum with all my strength. I was twice as slow as the big elf but I soon managed to get a rhythm going. He just stared at me as if I'd gone mad.

'What do you think?' I gasped between beats.

His scowl cracked, and for the first time I saw a grin spread over his face, 'No good.'

'Then show me. C'mon, you can't give up. This is probably just the beginning of our struggles. You've got to keep drumming. I'm going to bring Crazy Wolf back. Don't lose heart.'

Still beating, I handed him one stick. He paused then raised it upwards to bring it crashing down on the left drum, in time with mine, only twice as loud. After a few more beats, I gave him the other. Now he brought both sticks down, one after the other, in a deafening *Boom! Boom! Boom!*.

And when, moments later, I rode out of the village – it was to the rousing accompaniment of elf war drums.

CHAPTER EIGHT

★

Flight to Fort Mordecai

First I rode to the new fort, or what was left of it, to inspect the damage. I was careful not to go too close as the place was crawling with sky-cavalry troops.

Even from a distance I could see that it looked pretty badly damaged. The entire perimeter stockade was pocked with gaping holes and one of the guard towers had completely collapsed. I imagined it had to be just as bad on the inside with the buildings, stables and soldiers quarters hit too. But what had done this? Whatever it was, they were trying to mimic the powerful elf magic of a medicine mage. The destruction of the fort, backed up by the sheriff's testimony about the Gatlans' wagon, had as good as put a rope around my uncle's neck. This had to be that smelly wolfer woman's idea. I was sure she had something to do with it, though I knew Imelda couldn't have conjured a thunderball herself as only a fully fledged medicine mage like my uncle has such power.

A few sky-cavalry soldiers spotted me snooping around and began to ride over so I decided to make tracks.

It was a long, hard flight for Moonshine to the top of the Mid-Rock, climbing all the time. But she was more than capable. I'd learned over the years that there wasn't too much Shy couldn't do.

As we neared the top of the rock I gazed down at the wisps of cloud and mist and saw the landscape of the eastern arm: forests, rivers, hills, towns and villages. It seemed so vast; from up here it looked as though there was more than enough room for everyone.

Finally the rock's edge came into view, and flying over the precipice we found a little creek flowing with invitingly clear water. We landed and I set foot on the Mid-Rock for only the second time in my life.

Moonshine had a well-earned drink while I stared at the scorched landscape.

The Mid-Rock was the biggest, flattest part of the

Great West Rock but it was quite a barren, bleak place and had little of the lush green forest and grasslands of the two arms, especially the eastern arm. The sun beat down ferociously, baking the ground like the crust of a chokecherry pie. A clattersnake slithered noisily past my heel, startling me.

I stared out into the sky that stretched as far as the eye could see and thought about the upper world. I knew I couldn't ascend in a trance like my uncle but, standing quietly for a moment, I asked for the Great Spirit to help me find the right words for the high sheriff – the right words to help free my uncle.

We rode inland, soon arriving at the outskirts of Mid-Rock City. We passed close to the snake-bellied troll quarter, but all was quiet as the trolls sleep during the day and awake to cause mayhem during the night.

Finally we arrived at the fort.

Fort Mordecai is encompassed by a thick timber stockade, which in turn is surrounded by a deep ditch with sharp, wooden spikes protruding from it, and high soil and boulder ramparts. At each corner stood lofted lookout towers enclosing a cavalryman wearing a neat blue and yellow uniform and armed with a rifle.

I approached the sentry at the front gate and dismounted. 'I'm here to see the high sheriff,' I announced.

'And you are?'

'Name's Will Gallows.'

'Where you from, Will?'

'Oretown.'

'Wait a minute, I remember you, don't I?'

'I dunno,' I said, though his face was familiar.

'You're that kid from way back. Came here about the trouble in Deadrock with that little dwarf who works in the kitchen here,' he sneered.

Then it clicked. 'An' you're that guard who thought that Sheriff Slugmarsh was the best sheriff Oretown ever had.'

With a jerk the grin dropped off the guard's face and he clenched his fists. 'Watch your mouth, kid.'

I was in no mood for this interrogation at the guard hut but I had to get inside and that meant I had to be careful not to annoy him too much.

'Like I say, I need to speak to the high sheriff urgently.'

'No chance, he's busy dealing with an important security matter.'

'The attack on the new fort, I know, that's what I need to see him about.'

'Well he's busy questioning an elf suspect.' I saw him make a point of staring at my ears, craning his neck to look at both sides of my head until, with a sneer, he added, 'We lost three good men down there last night. Somehow I don't think he's gonna want to see the like o' you, kid.'

My mouth dropped open. I couldn't believe he was treating me like the men in the saloon had. Making out I was worthless because of my elf blood. What was happening to folk on the rock?

'Reckon he should be the judge of that. I've ridden all the way from the eastern arm, least you could tell him I'm here. I don't mind waiting.'

'Get lost, half-breed.'

'I'd do as he says, 'less you want me to tell the high sheriff 'bout that little high rollin' game of snake poker you an' your buddies were enjoyin' on duty while he was away on business the other day.'

I spun round, recognising the voice instantly – Jez!

The guard gasped. 'How'd you know 'bout that?'

'Bin livin' in this fort long enough that there ain't much I don't know about what goes on 'tween these four ramparts. Now, are you gonna stand aside or am I gonna have to spill the beans?'

'Other troops aren't gonna be happy 'bout an elf kid strollin' 'bout the fort. Not after what *his* people been up to.'

'There ain't nothing proved and he won't be strollin' 'bout the fort. He'll stay with me till the high sheriff's free to see him.'

With a growl, the guard moved out of my way, following me with a cold stare as I led Moonshine into the fort.

Jez almost bowled me over with a running hug then did the same to Moonshine, caressing my horse's neck.

'Sure is good to see you, Will. You too, Moonshine. I heard what happened – that's why you're here, ain't it?'

I nodded, wondering how much she knew.

'What have you heard?'

'That the fort was destroyed and three guards were killed by arrows. They say they have the elf who did it an' that he'll hang 'fore the week's out.'

My stomach lurched at the mention of hanging. 'Jez, they think Crazy Wolf did it. It's my uncle they'll hang before the week's out!'

The blood drained from Jez's cheeks and her eyes widened like a marsh toad's. 'But that's crazy.'

We both glanced over at the grinning guard who had a hand to his throat pretending to choke. 'Come on, let's get outta here.'

Jez's room was the one I'd stayed in with her last time we were at the fort and she took me straight there.

I told Jez everything. About the Gatlans' cattle tramping the elf corn fields, about the thunderball my uncle conjured, about the elf council meeting, about nearly being roasted by a thunder dragon, about the meeting in the Trunk and Arms – and how the Gatlans were plotting, with the help of Imelda Hyde the wolfer, to get rid of the medicine mage. I finished by telling her about Uncle Crazy Wolf's arrest.

'I don't know how the Gatlans did it, Jez, and, though it kills me to say it, it was the most crookedly brilliant thing they could've done. By attacking the fort, they've got rid of the most powerful tribesman on the arm as well as turning the sky cavalry against the elves. The cavalry'll probably turn a blind eye now if the Gatlans do raise an army against Gung Village, or worse, they might even join them.

'Have you seen the fort?'

'Yeah, it's a ruin, lookout tower's collapsed and—'

I broke off as the door flew open and a bunch of sky-cavalry soldiers stormed into the room. Seconds later I found myself staring down the barrels of three rifles.

'Hands in the air, boy!'

Jez screamed, 'What in spirit's name do you think you're doing, bursting into my room . . .?'

A skinny trooper pointed a rifle at her head. 'You too, hands up. Your boyfriend's trespassin' on cavalry premises.'

An officer pushed them out of the way as he entered the room. 'Put down your weapons, lads. Can't you see the boy's not armed?'

'That sort don't need guns,' snarled one of the soldiers. 'They can do that hocus pocus, same as what destroyed the fort.'

Jez was almost in tears. 'This is my fault, captain,' she choked, then glowered at the skinny trooper. 'I let

137

him in; he's a good friend of mine come to see the high sheriff.'

I recognised the captain. I was sure he had ridden with us months ago to seal the deep mines.

'Captain, it's me, Will Gallows.'

'Ah, I thought I knew you. I remember you fought bravely against the trolls that day in the mine tunnel. But what you doing here now? Elves ain't welcome on a day like today.'

I stood up straight. 'Captain, I'd like to speak with the high sheriff a few minutes, that's all I ask.'

'What about?'

'About the fort, my uncle is innocent.'

'Your *uncle*?' He paused, his brow furrowing, then added, 'You mean to tell me you're related to that elf wizard?'

I nodded.

'Look, on account of how you acted down those mines I'll tell the high sherriff you are here, Will Gallows, but I cannot promise he will see you.'

'I'm much obliged to you, sir,' I said.

I waited with Jez in silence, and when the captain returned minutes later he said, 'Come with me, Will.'

Jez tried to follow us but the captain glared at her. 'Not you. He'll see Will alone.'

I went outside with him, past a cluster of one-storey, wooden buildings. We passed small groups of cavalrymen busying themselves with the duties of the biggest and most important fort on the West Rock: cleaning rifles, pistols and sabres, repairing a damaged cart, and lugging bags of food supplies and equipment.

The captain knocked on the door of a small cabin and disappeared inside. He returned after a while to tell me the high sheriff would see me, and then he left.

Inside the cabin I took off my hat then stood squinting in the bright sunlight that poured in from the far window. A tall figure stood with his back towards me, silhouetted against the window. He wore a knee-length dark coat, and when he turned I noticed that his hair and moustache had paled from grey to almost white since I'd last seen him.

'It's good to see you again, Will. Though I must say I am surprised to find you are connected to the man we have arrested.'

'He didn't do it.'

'Because he's your uncle?'

'Because I was with him all night.'

'You were with him where?'

'In his tepee, in Gung-Choux Village. I'd gone to warn him that the Gatlans were plotting against him.' I told the high sheriff about the meeting in the Trunk and Arms saloon. As I spoke, he ran a hand slowly from his forehead to his chin.

'So you're saying the attack on the fort is all part of some elaborate plan by the Gatlan brothers to discredit the elf folk and win the support of the sky cavalry?'

'Precisely. They've been plotting to somehow get rid of my uncle, knowing it will crush the spirits of the whole elf tribe and make them easier to defeat in battle. The Gung-Choux braves are armed mainly with bow and arrows and spear, which are no match for six-shot blasters.'

'And how do you explain the attack itself? Surely you must agree that it bears all the hallmarks of a thunderball attack, as described by the sheriff of Dugtown. He says that only days ago your uncle destroyed the Gatlans' wagon in a similar display of magic. There isn't a weapon on the rock capable of such awesome power. This attack is practically a declaration of war!'

'No, please! The elf folk do not seek conflict. I don't know how the Gatlans did it, but I'll find out.'

'Look, Will, my hands are tied. You are a good kid, and your pa was the best deputy sheriff Oretown ever had. I'm just sorry that you of all people had to get caught up in this. Your uncle will get a fair trial in Mid-Rock courthouse, I'll see to that. You, of course, can testify that he was with you that night, maybe save him from the gallows. But now, if you'll excuse me, I have some business to see to.'

He ushered me towards the door.

'Can I see him?' I asked.

'Don't see why not. He's in Mid-Rock City jail. You ever been there?'

'No.'

'I'll get one of my men to take you over, but I don't want you in there any longer than five minutes, y'hear?'

'Yes, sir. Thank you.' He opened the door for me and I walked outside. 'I'm going to prove he's innocent.'

I had only just got back to Jez's room when she sprang off her bunk. 'I'm coming with you,' she said. 'I've asked the head cook and she's fine with me taking a few days off. It's OK with you, ain't it, Will?'

'Are you kidding? I'd be glad of the help. But are you sure? I've gotta feeling whoever did this won't like it when we start pokin' our noses in.'

She gave me the sort of look made me wish I hadn't wasted my breath asking the question. I nodded, grinning. 'Guess you're sure then.'

I hung around in Jez's room for a while until there was a knock on the door. Jez opened it and the guard we'd had a run in with at the fort entrance stood there grinning.

Jez shot him a testy glance. 'Not you again,' she wailed.

'Could say the same myself. What did I do to deserve gettin' lumbered with you kids?'

I pulled on my hat. 'Guess it's your lucky day. C'mon, let's get going.'

I checked in on Moonshine in the fort stable to tell her what was happening. Then we followed the guard, on foot, out of Fort Mordecai, down the hill and into the city. The sun was searing hot, as it always seemed to be on the Mid-Rock. We passed by the troll quarter and with its squashed-together buildings it reminded me of Oretown; the streets were deserted.

'Your uncle's in big trouble,' the guard commented

as we passed Mid-Rock City gallows tower, the noose swinging in the breeze. I felt a knot of bile rise in my chest as I realised that if they found Uncle Crazy Wolf guilty, that's where he'd end his days.

'He was set up. Though, like everyone else, I don't expect you to believe me, so if you'll just take us to the jailhouse.'

'No need to get all shirty, young fella. That's it up ahead.'

Mid-Rock City jailhouse was a drab-looking stone building in need of a fresh coat of paint. It had a narrow door and an even narrower barred window.

The guard entered first and we followed him inside. The interior consisted of a long four-celled cage running the length of one half of the building. The other side of the jailhouse was bare except for the jailer's desk and chair. The jail keeper rose as we entered, cocking the trigger of his gun, but he uncocked it when he noticed the sky cavalry uniform the guard wore.

'How many you got for bed and breakfast this week, ol' timer?' the guard asked.

'Got me a full house.' The jailer grinned. 'Eight killers, all for the rope: whip-tails, humans, snake-bellies, oh, and you'll never believe it – elves too!'

But there were only four cells! The guard must have noticed my puzzled look and whispered, 'The ol' man's eyes are as crossed as a snake-poker player's fingers, he's only got four prisoners.'

The jailer turned and I saw that both his eyes faced in towards his nose in an unusual expression. I wondered how secure a jail could be with a cross-eyed jailer.

'What can I do for y'all?' he said, looking me up and down – or both of me, as I figured he'd be seeing double.

'Got some kids here keen to visit your newest inmate, the murderin' elf wizard,' the guard explained.

'Elves. Y'mean elves, got me a coupla them in the bottom cell.'

'Yeah, whatever.' He groaned. 'For five minutes and not a minute more.'

The jailer directed his unruly pupils towards Jez nodding. 'I see, visitors for the elves, huh? Don't get many elves checkin' in here, and *killer* elves, well now, that's rarer still. Can't remember ever havin' killer elves behind these rusty bars.'

The guard grunted then, taking a seat behind the jailer's desk, he opened a drawer and pulled out a

bottle of Boggart's Breath whiskey and put his feet up. 'Like I say, five minutes.'

'They're in the bottom cell. Follow me.'

We followed the jailer to the end cell, past a snoring troll and a whip-tail goblin. In the cell next to my uncle, a cowboy sat on the edge of his bed, a white-toothed grin on his face.

'Those two grinnin' bandits are the quick-draw Crawford brothers,' the jailer explained. 'Though unfortunately for them, their draw is a lot quicker than their horses. The sheriff caught them ridin' off with a bag of cash from the Mid-Rock City bank.'

'Hope you got something tasty on the menu tonight, we're both starving,' the outlaw said with a wink. I guessed he'd be getting two meals a day.

Finally we came to the last cell which was furnished like the others. It had a single bed and a wooden bedside table with a jug of water and a book on it. Uncle Crazy Wolf sat on a stone ledge, his hands cuffed behind his back and his feet locked to a ball and chain. I was furious. No one else was chained in this manner and I complained to the jailer.

'Orders of the high sheriff. No one else can do

magic in this jail house. Apparently they destroyed a sky cavalry fort single-handed.'

'He was nowhere near the fort. I was with him in his tepee in Gung-Choux Village the night it was destroyed.'

Uncle Crazy Wolf looked up at us, 'Will! Jez! What are you doing here? You should not have come; they could frame and arrest you too.'

'We're gonna get you out of here,' I said.

Jez nodded. 'Yeah, don't worry, we'll find the real culprits and put *them* behind bars.'

Uncle Crazy Wolf looked downtrodden. I'd never seen him like this before. His face paint was streaked where his tears had run.

'This is the great darkness the elders warned of, and it is a darkness of the worst kind for I am powerless – powerless when the tribe needs me most.' He looked me in the eye. 'But you, Will, and young Jez here, you are two glimmers of light in this darkness. The spirits spoke of this too. You, Will, must become the village medicine mage in my absence. You must make use of everything I have taught you, all the many strands of elf magic: healing, spirit mediation and trances, rune-casting, fireball conjuring, arrow bending. And you

147

must rally the tribe and not let their spirits fall.'

I felt my jaw drop open. I couldn't believe my uncle thought I could take over as medicine mage. 'I will, Uncle Crazy Wolf. I'd consider it an honour. I told the chief I'm going after the Gatlans and I won't stop until I've uncovered the truth.'

'Good.' He sighed. 'I only wish I'd had time to teach you more.'

I recalled the last few days at the village and how we'd crammed so much in; it was as though he'd known this was in front of him.

'I know enough for now,' I assured him.

'I wish there were some other way, it is a lot to burden young ones with; and all on top of worrying about your grandma too.'

'I'm doing it for her as much as anybody,' I said. 'If the conflict between ranchers and elf folk isn't sorted, won't be worth her while moving to the eastern arm, she'd be better off staying put.'

Crazy Wolf closed his eyes. 'I can still see the hatred in the cavalrymen's faces, it was chilling. It is like they are blinded by their hatred. Their assumption of my guilt clouds their reason. All they can see is the three

dead cavalrymen in boxes outside the undertakers.'
Opening his eyes he asked, 'Did you see the fort, Will?'

'Yeah, it's a ruin. One of the towers has completely collapsed. I spoke to the high sheriff but he just said you'll get a fair trial. And, worse, he said this whole incident is a declaration of war. I figure this'll end up in another attack soon enough. Time's running out. They're all in on it, backing each other up, even the sheriff of Dugtown. Looks like Imelda Hyde's evil idea has worked. The Gatlans are probably gloating, thinking they're unstoppable.'

'With the sky cavalry on their side, they're not far wrong. It will not be easy to ride against them.'

'Jez, Shy and me are a proven team, if we can beat snake-bellied bandits we can take on low-bellied ranchers.'

'Yeah,' said Jez, 'them Gatlans don't know what they're up against.'

Uncle Crazy Wolf smiled. 'I'm glad you came. Already I feel my spirit lifting. May the Great Spirit go with you.

'Time's up!' the guard called.

We said goodbye and the guard led us out.

CHAPTER NINE

★

The Troll with Crooked Teeth

'Wow, the damage is a lot worse than I imagined,' Jez gasped.

Jez and I had flown back to the scene of the attack to try and find out what had really happened. There were still a few cavalrymen around the wrecked fort, though not as many as earlier, but it meant I couldn't get up close.

'So, where do we start?' Jez asked.

'Whatever we do, we need to move quickly. You heard the high sheriff say he's treating this attack as a declaration of war, and I'll bet the sky cavalry will be making preparations for battle. They won't be waiting for the trial, that's for sure – I think they've already got their minds made up.'

Keeping an eye on the cavalrymen we poked around the outskirts of the fort, hunting for clues. But we found nothing.

'Forest's quite close by,' Jez pointed out. 'Maybe they hid whatever did this in the forest until nightfall and then struck.'

'But that's the key bit, what *did* do this?'

'Something powerful. A weapon of some sort.'

'But what kind of weapon could create this sort of havoc? I've sure never seen one.'

My eyes raked the front of the damaged stockade. Something was puzzling me. 'What do you notice about where the fort was destroyed?'

'I'd say it was hit pretty much all over. Why?'

'Not really. Look, most of the destruction is at the front of the fort: those ramparts, the log stockade and guard house. So I think that whatever did this was fired from a location facing the fort entrance.'

'Yeah, you're right. It had to be.'

We searched around the exterior of the fort, looking for wheel track marks. Whatever the Gatlans had used they would have had to drag it into position first. But there was no sign of any tracks.

Then I heard the faint whistle of the Flyer and an idea struck me – almost like I'd been hit by the Flyer itself.

Positioning myself with my back to the fort, I said, 'Turn round like this, Jez, an' tell me what you see.'

She did as I told her then frowned. 'Don't see anything 'cept for miles o' flat prairie land.'

'You sure?'

'That an' . . . an' the railroad!'

'Exactly. What would be the best way to shoot up the fort without leaving any tracks?' I said excitedly. 'Use the tracks that are already there – rail tracks!'

At that moment the Flyer thundered past, very close to the front of the fort.

'You mean . . .'

'Yup. That whatever did this could've been fired from the Flyer.'

Jez stared after the train. 'So that might be the *how*, but we still don't know the *what*.'

'Maybe the railroad boss can tell us more. Reckon he's gotta be worth a visit.'

'Then what are we waiting for?' said Jez, starting

back towards where Moonshine and her own horse stood nibbling on some grass. 'C'mon, we'll go to Mid-Rock City and track down the railroad boss.'

I smiled. '*Track* down the railroad boss, I like that.'

We rode to Phoenix Rise. By the time we arrived it was nearly nightfall so we decided to stable the horses and take the train to Mid-Rock City first thing in the morning. While at the ranch, we had a good hearty beef-stew dinner, and as we ate we updated Tyrone on Crazy Wolf's arrest.

Tyrone was shocked by the news. 'Whole Rock's gone crazy,' he said. 'I'm sleepin' with my rifle these nights, an' none of us are riding too near the Gatlans' place.'

'Well, they're not gonna get away with this. Jez and I are gonna prove to the high sheriff that the Gatlans are rotten evil liars.'

The next morning I packed a bag with some beef strips, a bottle of water and a pouch of magic healing herbs, not forgetting my blowgun and jar of frog poison. Tyrone said he'd look after Jez's mare and keep an eye out for Moonshine's return.

Moonshine flew both of us to Dugtown station where the Flyer was shunting into the station as we arrived. 'Thanks, Shy. We'll be back soon, hopefully with a few clues as to what's going on.'

'I could fly you, save you the fare.'

I stroked her nose. 'You've flown plenty this last week, Shy. Get rested up. I figure you're gonna need all the strength you can muster over the coming days – we all are. Plus Jez and I have got an idea that the Flyer might somehow be caught up in all this so we wanna travel on it – check things out from close range.'

Jez and I took a seat in a carriage near the back and stared through the grubby window. The train got underway, *clickety-clacking* along the track, and it wasn't long until we passed the ruined fort. I gazed at the holed, damaged stockade, and thought of my uncle stuck in jail, worrying what was going to happen to him next.

154

And then the fort was gone and we were steaming over the bridge that connected the eastern arm to the Mid-Rock.

Jez fiddled with the little scorpion pendant around her neck.

'Remember when you gave me this?'

'The mine vents in Deadrock – how could I forget?'

'I ain't ever taken it off, y'know? Call it my good-luck charm.'

'Sure hope it brings us luck when we get to Mid-Rock City. We need as much as we can get right now.'

I'd forgotten just how big Mid-Rock City station was until the Flyer squealed to a stop beside the station platform: four rail tracks wide with a large terminal building containing a waiting room, saloon, toilets, offices and a stage coach depot for those folk who were journeying on to other parts of Mid-Rock.

Passing a newspaper stand, my eye caught the headline of the *Mid-Rock City Times*:

Mid-Rock City Times

Fears Grow for Crumbling Western Arm

I bought a copy of the newspaper. 'Look at this, Jez. Says here that the quakes are coupl'a times a day and that another big chunk o' rock broke off and fell into the Wastelands.'

I thought of Yenene, probably still sitting in her rocking chair while chunks of Phoenix Creek crashed down all around her. She was so stubborn. Why wouldn't she just leave it all behind for a fresh start? I felt guilty that I hadn't gone to tell her about her brother yet, but I figured saving him from the gallows was more important right now.

'Yenene's gotta change her mind an' leave soon, Will, while there's still a chance.'

We headed for a door marked OFFICE beside the saloon.

As we entered I was surprised by how dimly lit it was inside. The blinds were pulled on the windows, and the mostly human rail clerks were using saddlewood lamps perched on their desks to work by.

A fat troll in a brown waistcoat with a gold watch chain hanging from the pocket stood rummaging in a filing cabinet as we came in. Yenene said Mid-Rock trolls were just gangsters in suits and this one sure fitted the bill.

'We'd like to speak with the railroad manager, please.'

'You're speaking to him. Who are ya?' he asked, flashing a mouthful of yellow, crooked teeth.

'Will Gallows, an' this here's Jez. We'd like to talk to you about what happened at the fort.'

'You would? Well, I'd like to help you but I'm busy trying to run a railroad company.' He took a file out of the cabinet and noisily slammed the drawer shut. I glanced at Jez who was frowning.

'We realise you're busy, sir. It's just we'd sure appreciate a moment of your time.'

As he tucked the file under his arm, I noticed something move beneath his waistcoat, and a shiver ran up my spine. He was a snake-bellied troll. That explained the dim light. Snake-bellies hate sunlight. Most of them sleep during the day, and I wondered what he was doing up at this time. I figured maybe with running the railroad he had to be at the station, especially with the majority of trains running during the day. Last time I'd been this close to a snake-bellied troll was when I'd confronted Noose Wormworx, the most wanted troll on the Rock.

This troll now strode to a door with a sign nailed to it, which read in gold letters:

HOX SWILLET
MANAGER

He went inside. I expected him to slam the door like he'd slammed the cabinet drawer but he left it open, so I gestured to Jez and we followed him in.

It was the biggest office I'd ever seen, and had an enormous desk situated in front of a window with its shutters closed. There was a leather sofa and fancy carved wooden cabinets with bottles of Boggart's Breath and glasses on top, and a glass tank with a branch in it. But it was the object in the middle of the office that really caught my eye.

It was a scale model of the top of the eastern arm. I was pretty sure of this as it wasn't long ago that I'd been staring in awe at the real thing when I'd ridden Moonshine to Fort Mordecai: rolling hills, tiny trees and towns and villages, even the rivers were painted in bold blue paint, twisting across the model like a clattersnake. I'd never seen anything like it before. My admiration seemed to annoy the manager who grunted.

'You kids just come here to nose around my office?'

I didn't answer. I was still examining the model. I'd noticed that the newest rancher town of Blackwater, which I had only flown over once on Shy, had rail track running through it. 'Model's pretty neat, though

Blackwater doesn't have a railroad service.'

He grinned a big crooked-toothed grin. 'Not yet it don't,' he said. 'This here's a vision of the future, boy, our expansion plans for the eastern arm.'

'Wait a second, didn't the high sheriff block that proposal as it cuts through the Chokewoods and elf farmland?'

'Not entirely, it's still under negotiation.' At this the troll dropped into his seat and puffed, 'Now, about this fort?'

HOX SWILLET
MANAGER

'My uncle's been arrested by the sky cavalry, charged with the attack on the eastern arm's new fort, but he's been set up. And I wondered, as the Flyer's midnight service to the West Woods would've passed the fort that night, if anything unusual was reported by the driver or conductors?'

He'd been staring at me as I spoke, and now he tilted his head to one side. 'I knew there was something puzzling me about you, kid. You're a half-breed, ain't ya?' I heard a faint hiss from under his waistcoat then the head of a snake appeared and fixed me with its beady eye, tongue flickering.

I didn't like him steering away from my question, but I answered anyway. 'My pa was human and my ma was a green-skinned elf.'

'I see,' he said, quickly tucking the snake back inside.

'Was anything reported?' Jez urged.

'Not to me it weren't.'

He strolled to a glass tank beside a row of filing cabinets. When we'd first entered the office I'd been mildly curious about it, but the model of the eastern arm had deflected my interest. The tank contained a

160

piece of dead branch and it was only
when I looked for a second time
that I noticed something
coiled around it, leering at
me with hypnotic yellow
eyes, tongue flickering –
another snake. But this one wasn't attached to Hox's
belly – it was a venomous rock snake. Hox opened a
small container sitting near the tank and, to my disgust,
took out a shrivelled finger! He lifted the lid of the tank
and dropped it inside. The snake struck, swallowing
the meal whole.

'As far as I know the midnight service to the West
Woods ran without incident,' he went on, 'though the
driver did report a few tremors on the western arm and
a drunken brawl in one of the carriages over a snake-
poker game.' He glanced at the rock snake. 'Look, if
you want to hang on, I could have a word with the
office staff?'

I nodded. 'We'd appreciate that.'

Hox left and I glanced at Jez.

'What do you think?'

'Reckon he's lying through those crooked teeth.'

'Y'see what he fed the snake?'

'Looked like a finger. Seeing that snake sent a shiver big as an ogre down my neck.'

'Me too.'

Next thing, I felt something slither past my leg.

'*Aaahh!* The snake!' I yelled. I noticed that the lid sat crooked on the tank and the snake had crawled through the gap. There was no cure for the poisonous rock-snake bite, and it was a horrible way to go: severe pain, vomiting, convulsions and then death.

Instinctively I kicked out my leg but only managed to shake the rock snake over to Jez and it quickly wrapped itself round her ankle before she too kicked it with a screech. The snake skittered across the office, turning to hiss at us. It wasn't happy at being kicked around, and slithered back towards us, bearing its fangs hungrily.

I held out both palms and fixed the snake with a glare. 'One more slither and I'll fry you with a fireball, an' I'm not bluffing.'

The snake stopped dead, its tongue tasting the air. It stared hypnotically, probing my mind in a trance-like state, detecting if I was lying like it did during snake-poker games when it tried to spot a bluffer. Rock snakes didn't usually critter chatter but it could still understand me. I wished I could get it to tell me what sort of things had been going on in Hox's office of late. Maybe it knew something about the attack on the fort.

'What kind of snake is it?' Jez asked, knife in hand.

'A rock snake – deadly poisonous. Don't move a muscle.'

I'd bought myself a bit of time to conjure the fire spell but found it hard to focus. I was conscious of both Jez and the snake staring at me expectantly and it threw off my concentration. It was the same back at Gung Village when I figured I'd got a piece of magic just right, then I'd go to show Uncle Crazy Wolf and I couldn't do it.

As though sensing my hesitation, the rock snake edged forward on its scaly belly, at the same time rearing up until it was waist height. I was suddenly aware of just how big it was, much bigger than the one I'd seen in Deadrock the night I'd played snake-poker. Hox had sure been feeding it well with shrivelled fingers and spirit knows whatever else.

'Will, look out, it's gonna strike!' Jez screamed.

I felt the sweat on my forehead trickle down to the tip of my nose. Then, still not taking my eyes off the snake, my hands began to burn and a waif of smoke spiralled into view, until, with a *whoosh*, a globe of fire erupted from my skin and crackled angrily just above my palms.

Jez gasped. 'Wow. Looks like your uncle's doing a fine job teaching you elf magic.'

I smiled as the snake began to back up, now hissing with fear instead of anger, I figured.

But I figured wrong. This snake wasn't giving up without a fight. Maybe it had guessed that I didn't really want to fry it. With a blood-curdling hiss. It struck, mouth gaping, bearing sabre-sharp fangs. Instinctively I propelled the fireball forward so it engulfed the snake's scaly head. There was a horrible sizzling noise, accompanied by the stink of burning snake-skin, as the rock snake slumped in a heap at my feet.

'Ye-haaa! You cooked it good,' Jez cried.

'I didn't wanna kill the stupid snake – I only wanted to scare it off.'

'You scared it, all right, scared it to death.' She grinned.

We were still staring at the charred remains when Hox burst back in. 'What the heck . . .?! What've you done to my snake?'

'What's the matter?' Jez sneered. 'Surprised to see us both still alive? Y'know, you really should be more careful – you left the lid off the tank.'

I frowned. 'Yeah, an' if I didn't know any better, I'd swear you did it on purpose.'

Hox's face reddened. Belly snakes appeared from under his shirt to hiss at me – as if I hadn't had enough of snakes for one day. Furiously he clenched his fists then bellowed, 'Why, I shoulda just put a bullet in you both – woulda been far quicker.'

He grabbed me by the collar and slammed me against the wall.

'S . . . so you did just try to kill us then?' I gasped.

His fist was pressing against my throat, choking the very life out of me. 'Maybe I did, maybe I'm still gonna . . . for killing my rock snake.'

'Put him down!' Jez screamed, unsheathing her knife.

The door opened suddenly and a grey-haired human lady, who I recognised as one of the office

166

workers, with a pen behind her ear, stuck her head round the door. 'Sorry, sir, but there's a signal problem on platform one . . . Is everything OK, sir?'

'Everything's fine!' Hox boomed, relaxing his grip on my collar. I slid down the wall. 'Can't *you* see to it?' he bellowed so loud that the other office workers began to peer inside to see what was going on. 'It's the middle of the day out there. Find one of the engineers to fix the signal problem.'

'We'll see ourselves out,' I said grabbing Jez by the arm and squeezing past the grey-haired lady. We ran through the office and onto the platform.

'Wow,' Jez panted. 'We've only just started trying to discover who framed your uncle and already people are trying to kill us.'

'Well, Hox knows more than he's tellin' us, I'm sure of it.'

'What are you thinking?'

'About that model of the new rail link to Blackwater. The chief mentioned it, saying he'd blocked the proposal as it ran through the Chokewoods and elf farmland.'

Jez gasped. 'So maybe the railroad manager is sore at the elves for stopping his new route. Sore enough to help the Gatlans mount an attack on the fort by letting them use his trains to do it?'

'Perhaps. Later, when the Flyer gets in, we should try to get a closer look at it. Maybe examine some of the freight cars and carriages. But now I wanna check out something else.'

Jez and I headed away from the station into the city streets.

I stopped a passer-by, enquiring, 'Is there a gunsmith's in town?'

The man pointed down the street. 'Take a left at the bank and you can't miss it.'

The gunsmith's store was a tall skinny shop wedged between the undertaker and the doctor. I smiled thinking that was kind of an appropriate place for it to be.

A sign on the door read:

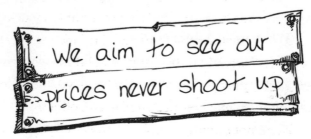

We aim to see our prices never shoot up

We entered the shop only to see a broad-shouldered man raise the barrel of an enormous rifle and discharge both rounds directly at us.

The noise was deafening. Jez screamed.

Heart pounding, I waited to feel the searing pain of a bullet, but none came and, looking down at the dust cloud near my feet, I caught sight of the man's real target: a big fat dust rat, lying on its back – dead.

'A female,' Jez muttered coolly. 'Male won't be too far away.'

'You both OK?' the gunsmith puffed, wiping the sweat from his brow. 'Sorry 'bout that but that sucker's been giving me the run around all day.' He held up the rifle. 'Got a special on these today, good long-range on them for hunting pick-tooths. Mind you, you don't look like wolfers to me; don't smell like 'em, either.'

'We're not buying.' I took out the newspaper. 'You heard about the new fort being smashed up?'

'Who hasn't? You'd need to have your head buried in the sand not to have heard.'

'Folks are saying there isn't a weapon on the rock capable of putting holes in solid timber like that, is that true?'

'Simple answer: yes. From what I can tell, of course.'

'What do you mean?'

'I mean I haven't seen the damage.'

Jez took out her little bone-handled knife and drew a large circle in the dirt floor of the shop.

'The holes were about that size,' she explained. 'They were dotted around the perimeter wall with a couple causin' one of the guard towers to collapse.'

The gunsmith studied the circle for a while then, reaching behind the counter, he took out a thick-barrelled weapon and took aim towards the back of the shop. There was a loud blast and, after the smoke cleared, a fist-sized hole appeared in the shop wall. I stifled a grin, wondering how long the gunsmith's shop would stay standing if he kept testing all the guns on the walls.

'That's the biggest hole you're gonna make from anything in my shop, an' it's the best darn gunsmith's on the entire West Rock.'

'Well, something made those holes,' Jez remarked.

Replacing the gun back under the counter the gunsmith said, 'Heard it was an elf wizard done it in protest at the sky cavalry building the fort smack in the middle of their land. They call him a medicine wizard . . .'

'Mage,' I corrected. 'My uncle, and he was nowhere near the fort that night, he was set up.'

Behind us the door opened and Buck Gatlan walked in. He took off his hat and rested it against his fat gut.

'Well, well, what have we here?'

'You won't get away with this, Buck Gatlan,' I snarled.

'Get away with what?'

'You know darn well. You set up my uncle like you said you would at the saloon meeting.'

'You're way off, half-breed, thinkin' I'd slay sky cavalrymen when in a few days we're gonna be ridin' flank-to-flank with them into battle against the real culprits – the Gung-Choux elf tribe!' He snarled. 'Oh, didn't you hear? It's confirmed; we got the full support of the high sheriff of Mid-Rock City. Reckon they'll probably hang your uncle 'fore the week's out.'

'My people had nothing to do with that attack. You're a filthy rotten liar and I'm gonna prove it.'

Buck drew his pistol, pointing it at my head.

'Not the smartest move on the rock, killin' the main suspect's nephew,' Jez said calmly, 'bound to raise a bushy grey eyebrow or two in Fort Mordecai.' She sure had a knack of keeping a cool head in times of trouble.

Buck's gaze darted between Jez and me. 'Swear one day I'm gonna put a bullet in you, half-breed.'

'S'just a kid, Buck,' the gunsmith piped up. 'He ain't worth it.'

'He ain't worth it, all right.' Buck re-holstered his six-shot blaster and strode to the counter. 'You got that delivery of cold hard steel I ordered?'

172

'Out the back. You'll need a wagon, there's some heavy metal in those crates.'

He nodded. 'Already hired one to haul 'em to the Flyer.'

'Hope it ain't got no holes in it, like yours,' I said, grabbing Jez. We darted through the door before Buck had a chance to go for his six-shot again.

We hung about some, spying on Buck for a while. When he came out he took the cart round the back of the shop. We followed him and watched as he loaded on the wooden crates.

'More guns,' said Jez.

I heard the Flyer. 'C'mon, Flyer's rolling in. Let's go back and take a look round the station.'

CHAPTER TEN

★

On the Roof of the Flyer

Jez and I hurried to Mid-Rock City station.
The Flyer was in and passengers were busily getting on and off, lugging their cases.

We headed past the engine, coal cart, fancy first-class carriages and standard carriages to the back of the train where the freight carts were coupled. I counted seven altogether, including horseboxes. Moonshine hated riding in the horsebox – she said it was stuffy and there wasn't even a window to look out. I think Moonshine would've preferred first class, if they'd let her in. Railroad workers were unloading goods down ramps that splayed onto the platform.

'What are you thinkin'?' Jez asked.

'That I'm not sure what we're looking for,' I said

deflated. I was beginning to wonder if my hunch was even right. Maybe the attack had nothing to do with the Flyer, maybe the Gatlans had destroyed the fort in some other way. My mind went back to what we'd seen earlier at the fort, the lack of tracks. No, it had to be something to do with the Flyer – how else could they have done it?

'Will, look!' Jez exclaimed pointing to the last wooden freight carriage. 'Funny ain't nobody using this one.'

I tried the handle but then noticed a big metal padlock swinging on the door bar.

'It's locked up real good.'

We tried peering through cracks in the door but it was pitch-dark inside the windowless freight carriage. What was in there? Why was no one loading stuff onto it?

I asked a train attendant why it wasn't being used, but he just shrugged his shoulders and wandered off.

'Somehow we've gotta find out what's inside that last car.'

'But how? The carriage is locked up like a safe full of gold.'

'We've gotta think.'

Just then the whistle for boarding blew loudly.

'C'mon, we'll think on board.'

We chose an almost-full carriage so there was no chance Buck would come in and we'd have to stare at his ugly face for the whole trip. We sat silently. The man opposite was reading the *Mid-Rock City Times* and that same headline about the crumbling western arm made me shudder.

Eventually there was a loud whistle and the Flyer got underway.

When we were steaming a path out of the city the conductor entered the carriage. My face must've lit up cos Jez tapped my knee.

'What is it, Will?'

'I know him. He's a green-skinned elf. Met him last year when I was riding the railroad down to Deadrock. D'you remember I told you about him? He was apprenticed to a medicine mage when he was young but he gave it up to work for the railroad. Maybe *he* could get us into that carriage.'

The elf caught my gaze. I tipped my hat, but he ignored me and just carried on issuing a ticket to the man with the newspaper. I recalled how he'd conjured a flame to light the tunnel lamps with his bare hands. He turned to leave but I jumped off my seat and caught his arm. 'Wait. Remember me?'

The elf rolled a milky eye at me, a fraught expression on his face. He shook his head. 'Sorry, kid, but I don't reckon I do.'

'It was a while back, I s'pose, but I told you about my uncle . . .'

'Sorry, I don't know you,' he broke in, now becoming agitated. 'And if you'll excuse me . . .' And he slipped out of the carriage door as though he couldn't get away quick enough.

It bothered me how he'd acted. I remembered him as a friendly man, not rude or abrupt like this.

'What's eatin' him?' Jez remarked when I sat back down.

'Dunno, weren't expecting a reaction like that.'

'Probably just mad that he's a thousand years old and still has to work for a livin'.'

Then, to my surprise, he re-entered the carriage and handed me a ticket-sized piece of paper.

'I'm sorry, sir, but I forgot to give you your ticket.' He smiled and was gone.

I glanced at Jez who frowned back at me, then we both looked down at the piece of paper. A note, scribbled in shaky handwriting read:

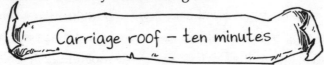

Carriage roof – ten minutes

The elf *had* remembered me. And he wanted to see me – but what for? Maybe he would have talked before but the compartment was too crowded. Maybe he knew something about the fort. I was bursting to find out but realised I must continue to act normally, so when the man with the newspaper peered over the top of his spectacles, I calmly folded the note and put it in my pocket.

Jez and I sat for a few minutes and then I nudged her. 'We should go check on Grandma.'

She nodded and we left the carriage. We continued down to the end of the corridor to a door with a sign saying:

DANGER
DO NOT OPEN

Without a second thought I slammed both hands on the door bar. We stood on a narrow boarding platform that had steps on one side and was bordered on the other three sides by a metal safety rail. The noise from the speeding train as the door opened was heart stirring. A ladder ran up the carriage end to the roof and I climbed it carefully, Jez at my heels. At the top I turned to help Jez, then we both scrabbled on hands and knees to grab hold of the rail that ran along the carriage-top. The wind gusted fiercely and I pulled my bandana up over my mouth. There was no sign of the elf conductor.

'Last time we did this you were on the run from that crazy whip-tail goblin,' Jez chuckled. She took a big gulp of air then, exhaling, she threw back her head, her hair blowing wildly like a sky-cavalry flag in the hands of a charging soldier. 'Ain't been up top like this for a while, I sort of miss it too.'

'Where is he?' I said, worrying that the elf might not come. Maybe he'd changed his mind. I was dying to know what was so important that he had to meet us on the roof.

At last I caught sight of his grey hair billowing at the top of the ladder. Jez and I both edged forward to lend a hand; the elf conductor looked even older than Grandma, and she was seventy-seven. I was surprised by how agile he was, though, as, spider-limbed, he crawled over the carriage-top to join us.

The wind gusted, and all of us were white-knuckled, clinging to the rail.

'I don't think I've seen the train so full of folk – there was no way I would've been able to speak with you privately.' He seemed anxious.

I didn't take my eyes from him as he peered over the side of the carriage, as though afraid some eavesdropper might have their head stuck out an open window. 'Then you do remember me – Will. Will Gallows?'

He smiled. 'Of course I remember you, Will, but no one must know. Especially not the railroad company – you'll understand why in a moment.'

I nodded. 'OK.'

The elf gave a long sigh. 'A great evil has been done to your uncle, the mage of Gung-Choux Village. I, as you know, was once an apprentice mage and I believe the spirits have ordained that I should see what I've seen and that I should meet whom I have met – that is you both.' He nodded to Jez, and I realised how rude I'd been not introducing her.

'I'm sorry, this is my good friend Jez. Jez this is . . .' I trailed off. He never had told me his name.

'My name is not important. I am pleased to meet you, Jez.'

'You read of the fort, the murders and my uncle's arrest?'

He nodded gravely. 'In horror and disbelief.'

'He's innocent; the whole thing is a set-up. I was with him in his tepee in Gung-Choux Village when it happened, his snoring kept me awake all night.'

The elf stared at me, pale eyes fixed on me, hair still billowing around his wrinkled face.

'I know,' he said slowly. 'If he had been at the fort that night I'd have seen him.'

I gasped, 'You were there?'

181

'Much mystery still shrouds what happened, but what I know I will tell you.'

I glanced over and saw we were crossing the bridge that linked the Mid-Rock to the eastern arm. If the wind picked up now we ran the risk of being blown over the edge into the gorge.

'The evening before it happened I had worked a double shift covering for a friend. My shift was almost over. The Flyer was climbing up from Deadrock. It was dark. As we crossed the western arm there was a quake – big one. I was sure the whole arm was finally gonna break off and plunge us all to our deaths.

'Anyway, whether it was out of relief at getting across safely, or just tiredness at working so many hours, or both, I don't know, what I do know is that in the darkness of the Mid-Rock tunnel I found a quiet carriage, lay down under the seat in the luggage space and went to sleep.

'I awoke much later to find it eerily quiet. We were in Mid-Rock City station. Conjuring a fingertip flame, I looked at my watch and realised that it would be half an hour before the next service – the midnight train. I'd got time to gather myself and sneak off the train without the boss knowing about my little snooze. But suddenly the train began to shunt forward. Getting up, I peered through to the next carriage only to see it was empty, and it struck me that the whole train was probably empty, except for the driver. It *had* to be empty, it was leaving half an hour early. But why?

'I was intrigued. Something wasn't right. The Flyer always runs like clockwork. I was annoyed at myself for sleeping and getting into this predicament. I wanted to go home, not travel all the way down the West Rock again, but I was curious to know what was going on.

'I waited, staring at the starry sky. We crossed the bridge onto the eastern arm. After a while I felt the train slow down. I conjured up a fingertip flame and checked my watch and realised that not enough time had passed for us to be in Dugtown yet. So why were we slowing?

'Minutes later we had completely stopped – stopped in the middle of nowhere.

The starlight revealed rolling hills to the west, and the start of the Chokewoods and the valley that ran all the way to the rock's edge. This was no train station – the only passengers at this stop would be a lone pick-toothed wolf and maybe a few bats.

'I heard voices followed by someone opening the freight carriage and a noise like the freight-car ramps being lowered. Then grunting, straining noises, wood cracking. It seemed we were taking on cargo. I hung out the window, squinting to try and see better, but I was too far forward. The bend in the track was obscuring my view.

'And then we were moving again. But only as far as the fort. Again the brakes squealed and we stopped. And then it happened.'

'What happened?' I gasped.

'A terrible noise, an explosion, like the roar of a mighty thunder dragon, then after a pause there was another and another and each time the train shook, like it did going over the western arm during a rock quake. There was lots of smoke too, smelled like gunpowder smoke.'

Jez and I stared at each other, open-mouthed. My heart hammered like a Gung-Choux war drum and an

184

ice-cold shiver shot up my back.

'It was dark but I could see the outline of the fort, I could hear the destruction, the cries of pain, the log stockade shattering under the fierce pounding from a weapon I could only imagine to be the stuff of nightmares.

'And then we were moving again. Leaving the scene of carnage, walls crumbling, soldiers dying. I'm standing trembling, trying to make sense of it all when next thing I feel something sharp in my back and hear a gruff voice threaten, "Dunno what hole you crawled out of, ol' timer, but if you wanna live the few years ya got left on this rock then you'll pretend you didn't see or hear anything unusual tonight, y'hear?"' The elf pulled down his collar exposing a fine red scar on his neck. 'He ran the blade across my throat, warned me that he'd cut it deeper next time if I told anyone. I was terrified. I wanted to tell, but whoever had threatened me didn't sound like he was bluffing. So I kept it all in. It's been eating me up inside. Then when I saw you, that's when I decided I couldn't keep it to myself any longer.'

'You done right, an' we won't breathe a word about this to anybody,' said Jez.

'That's for sure. What happened after that?' I asked.

'Whoever was responsible for the carnage had timed it so that the train got into Dugtown at its due arrival time, to the minute. Passengers got on and the service continued as normal. There must have been a different conductor on that night, or maybe they just gave the few folk that were on it a free trip.'

'Then whatever destroyed the fort was – or still is – aboard the Flyer, that's what we figured,' I gasped.

'And the crooked-toothed railroad boss is in it up to his fat neck,' Jez seethed. 'And he told us the midnight service passed off without a hitch.'

I asked the elf conductor about getting into the locked freight carriage, but he said it would be impossible to get hold of the key.

My gaze wandered over the elf's shoulder and I saw low hills in the distance and, to one side, a narrow valley with the Chokewoods encroaching from the right.

'We've gotta be near the place you say the Flyer stopped that night. Do you remember where it was?'

The elf followed my gaze then carefully checking his watch said, 'Yes. It was somewhere round the next bend in the track.'

Suddenly I had an idea. 'Reckon it's gotta be worth checking out. The train slow much rounding that bend?' I asked.

The elf nodded. 'A bit, why?'

I smiled. 'Cos a coupl'a passengers are getting off. You up for it, Jez?'

'No problem.'

'Only wish Shy was in the horsebox. Make it a whole lot easier.' I stared at the bare, rocky landscape patched with clumps of tangleweed and a few scorched, twisty trees. 'And less painful.'

'Tangleweed's fairly dense round here,' said the elf conductor. 'If you could find a big bunch of thick stuff and aim for that you'd probably walk away without a scratch. What are you going to do after that?'

'What you've seen proves the railroad are in on it. What we have to prove is that it wasn't magic destroyed the fort; that it was a weapon of some kind, fired from the Flyer during the night.'

We climbed down to the edge of the carriage roof, and my eyes raked the approaching landscape for a big bank of soft tangleweed.

'May the Great Spirit go with you both,' said the elf

conductor. 'These are dark days. I will also try and find out more of what the railroad company are up to.'

'Thank you.' I said, raising my hat.

Jez shook his hand vigorously, 'Goodbye, sir.'

'Pick your landing spot and jump as far away from the train as you can.'

Nearing the bend in the track, the Flyer's brakes squealed. That was our signal. The elf peered up ahead with his arm raised.

'Get ready!' he cried.

My heart pounded and I sucked in a few quick breaths of air. 'You all set, Jez?'

'Like a chokecherry jelly!'

The elf conductor dropped his arm. 'Here it is, now pick your spot and jump!'

We moved to the edge of the coupling.

'I'll go first!' I yelled, tossing my hat, my eyes fixed on a big, thick clump of green tangleweed. Taking a deep breath I jumped at an angle as far as I could, away from the carriage, hands protecting my head. Grunting, I landed on my side, the momentum causing me to roll like a log down the bank. When I stopped rolling I got up, dusted myself off, then looked round for my hat.

Jez was already on her feet and running towards me. 'You OK?'

'Yeah,' she beamed. 'To be honest, I'd forgotten how much fun it is doing stuff like that.'

The Flyer disappeared from our view, heading for its next stop – Dugtown.

'Well, let's make a start looking around. Least this time we know there might be something.'

We renewed our search for tracks with more vigour, sure that there had to be some trace of whatever had been loaded onto the Flyer that night. But I knew it wouldn't be easy. It was a big old rock top and the elf had only given us a rough idea of where the Flyer had taken on its mysterious load.

'OK, so if the Flyer stopped to take on cargo then there should be tracks close to the railroad. So let's refine our search to the trackside for now.'

We walked to where the track began to straighten out again but saw nothing.

'This is probably far enough,' I said. 'The elf said the train stopped on the bend. C'mon we'll double back, there has to be some trace of what happened that night.'

After scouring the landscape until our necks ached

Jez cried out, 'Found something!'

I hurried over. At her feet, etched into the baked earth, were cart tracks.

'Well done, Jez.'

'Look, there's hoof prints too.'

There wasn't a moment to lose and we set about following the tracks.

Up ahead the valley tapered into a narrow gorge. Jagged rock towered on either side of us. The gorge was no more than a wagon's-width wide, and towering rock closed in at the top to leave a thin scar of sky.

'The tracks seem to be leading us to the rock's edge.'

'I don't get it,' said Jez. 'This is completely desolate – there's nothing here.'

When we reached the other side of the gorge the terrain spread out again. The wind picked up, and this, along with the blue haze in the distance, told me we were nearing the rock's edge. Although the patch of ground we walked on was flat, to our left the landscape changed to low rolling hills, skirting the rock's edge.

And then the tornado struck.

CHAPTER ELEVEN

★

Menace in the Chokewoods

The tornado appeared out of nowhere, as they usually did on the West Rock: a towering grey mass of spinning cloud, ferociously ploughing the ground, ripping up trees and bushes and anything that got in its path.

'Quick, head for the woods!' I cried.

We took cover in the Chokewoods, the darkest, creepiest-looking forest I've ever seen. But it was either that or be sucked into the eye of the tornado, spun around like a sky-cowboy's lasso then spat back out onto the rocky ground.

The trees in the Chokewoods are easily the weirdest on the entire West Rock.

The roots of one species, not

content with burying deep into the earth and staying there, instead sprout back out of the ground, twist a few feet into the air then curve back into the earth. In this fashion they snake along the forest floor, intertwining with one another. In some places it's almost impossible to walk without tripping over them.

The storm raged, swirling near to the edge of the forest where we'd taken refuge. We both clutched a big snaking root as the worst of the tornado passed, shoving both legs under it and clinging on.

Finally the winds began to calm.

'C'mon, let's get outta here.' I went to get up but found I couldn't. 'Jez, help me, I'm stuck.'

The root had tightened around my legs, holding me fast. It wasn't my imagination; there was definitely something weird going on here.

Jez tried to pull me out but it was no good. The more I tried to wriggle free, the tighter the root held me. Then, to my horror, the root began to move in the earth, uncoiling round my legs, pulling me towards the bark of the tree. And it was then that I saw the cavernous hole in the old tree trunk, like some dark, gaping mouth.

'Jez, quick, do something! I think it's . . . it's trying to eat me!'

Jez, her eyes wide in terror, pulled out her little bone-handled knife and thrust it with all her strength into the root. There was a low, guttural, echoing roar, coming from deep inside the trunk as it released me – and I struggled free.

'What the heck was that?' I panted.

'It was like some crazy type of carnivorous tree.'

'This place gives me the creeps. C'mon, let's get out of here.'

As we walked I slowly realised we were taking an unusually long time to reach the edge of the woods.

'Reckon we should o' been out by now,' I said.

'Reckon so too,' said Jez.

A tiny bird stared at me from a gnarled tree branch, chirping loudly. I sighed. 'Which I guess means we're—'

'Lost,' Jez finished.

This was all I needed. Getting lost when we should be finding out what the Gatlans were up to and freeing Uncle Crazy Wolf before they dropped a noose around his neck. It was bad enough the tornado forcing us off the trail. Now the storm was bound to have covered over the tracks, meaning our best lead yet on what had destroyed the fort was gone.

'It's all these stupid trees, they're so similar – you can't keep track o' where you been.'

Suddenly I heard noises. Footsteps. No. Too heavy sounding. I stopped, turning my head, listening.

Thud! Thud! Thud!

'You hear that, Jez?'

Jez drew up beside me and listened. 'Yeah, someone's there.'

They were chopping sounds, the dull impact of an axe on wood, and they were coming from close by. I was curious to know what was making noises this deep inside what I'd figured was an uninhabited wood. I walked slowly through the trees towards a clearing.

The chopping grew louder and was joined by gruff voices; voices that took me back to the tin mine near Deadrock. That was where I'd last heard the sounds of many trolls working – and that was what confronted me as I stared into the gloomy clearing from the cover of a thick saddlewood tree.

There were about ten of them – snake-bellied trolls, from what I could see – busily working; swinging razor-sharp axe heads into the trunks of ancient chokewood and saddlewood trees: talking, cursing, laughing. Two burly trolls worked with a long double-handled saw, slicing deep into the bark of one of the twisty trees that had earlier trapped me under its roots. I noticed that the trolls had made sure to carve up the roots first so the tree couldn't harm them.

As I stared something hard struck the back of my head, through my hat. I heard myself cry out then, swathed in pain, I sank to my knees as everything went black.

I opened my eyes sometime later. My head throbbed and my vision was blurred. Blinking, I quickly realised I was still in the middle of the clearing with the trolls, but that they'd shrunk or I'd grown six feet taller while I was unconscious. Blinking again, I felt thick, taut rope dig into my arms and legs, and I realised that my new-found perspective was due to the fact I'd been tied to a saddlewood tree about a horse's height from the ground. Now I knew how Uncle Crazy Wolf felt tied up in jail. I glanced across the clearing and was horrified to see Jez bound in a similar fashion to a tree in front of me. A troll swung an axe into the bark below her feet, chopping down the tree.

I heard a troll voice murmur from somewhere behind me, 'It'll be ten times quicker when we get the new weapon, we can just blast the stupid trees out of the ground!'

The troll that was cutting Jez's tree, a big ugly one with a nose full of warts and arms thick as totem poles, noticed me come to and strode over, tapping the blunt edge of his axe against the palm of his hand.

'Head hurt, boy?' he sneered, and I noticed something wriggle under his shirt at his belly. Small beady eyes regarded me as the oily black head of a snake peered out through the gap between the troll's shirt buttons, tongue flickering.

'Who are you?' I groaned, the words making my head throb unbearably.

'The last troll you're gonna set eyes on 'less you tell me what you and your little dwarf friend here are doin' pokin' about the woods, spyin' on folk.'

He twirled the axe in the air, caught the handle, ran a thumb over the blade checking for sharpness, then to my horror swung it at my legs. For a heart-stopping moment I thought he was going to chop off my feet, but with a dull thud the axe head buried deep into the bark, a whisker below the heels of my boots.

Some of the other trolls eagerly clustered around, noticing our exchange and probably hoping to see some blood, but the big troll ordered, 'Back to work, there's no time for idlin'!'

Looking him in the eye, I cried, 'These woods belong to the Gung-Choux elves, you got no right to be felling trees!'

'You got no right to be felling trees.' The troll hurled the words back at me in an annoying squeaky voice. 'Got all the right on the rock, kid. Besides, since when does a rancher stick up for elf folk? Thought you'd be pleased to see progress is bein' made on the new eastern rail network.' Again he swung the axe fiercely into the tree and a wedge of bark splintered off through the air. 'Now, who are ya and what are ya doin' out here?'

I gasped. 'You're railroad workers, Hox's men?'

The troll nodded. 'You're lookin' at part of the clearin' that'll carry the new rail link to Blackwater and the edge lands.'

'But the planning permission for this hasn't been granted. The high sheriff blocked it in support of Chief Red Feather's protest that it would cause too much destruction and pollution to the Chokewoods. A new route will have to be proposed.'

'Ain't no other route an' Red Feather knows it. There's only one way to run a railroad to Blackwater an' it's through this forest. Now, what are you doing sneakin' around these woods, kid? Are you spyin' for the chief? Can't help but notice them fine pair of ears you're tryin' to hide under that cowboy hat. You ain't a real rancher. You're a half-breed, ain't ya? Reckon there ain't nothin' I hate as much as a half-breed.'

'I'm spying for nobody, if you must know. I'm out to clear my uncle's name for the attack on the new fort. You know anything about that?'

'Yeah, I know about it.'

'I heard your men talk of a weapon. What did they mean?'

'You're delirious, kid. Dunno what you're talkin' about.'

'You can't just chop your way through an ancient forest. The elf folk depend on it for their livelihood, and the wildlife for hunting.'

'My heart bleeds for your elf-critter friends but even they can't be so stupid not to realise that change is comin', progress is being made and Hox, and others like him, ain't gonna sit around all day waitin' for a bunch o' long-ears to start towing the line.'

'Progress! You call destroying a forest, killing all the wildlife and habitat, progress? You call not listening to folk who live here and have been living here for hundreds of years, progress?'

The troll took another great chunk out of the saddlewood trunk and I felt it lurch slightly forward, creaking like the bones of an old man. I swallowed hard, fighting back the thoughts of the whole thing crashing to the ground, squashing me on the forest floor, flatter than one of Yenene's pancakes.

I glanced over at Jez who stared back wide-eyed, struggling against her ropes, and for a second I tried to think how she would act in a situation like this.

She always kept a cool head. 'You really wanna add murder to the list of crimes the high sheriff's gonna bring you in for?' I asked.

'You don't know what you're talkin' 'bout, kid.' The troll grinned. 'The high sheriff's only pretendin' to care about the elf folk. And after what happened at the fort I know for a fact he's swingin' round to our way o' thinkin' quicker than I'm swingin' this here axe.'

'Tell me what really happened at the fort. You know, don't you?'

'Crazy old elf wizard destroyed it usin' some sort of ancient magic.'

'You're lying!'

With more venom he hacked another piece of wood from the tree. 'You're the liar, kid. You're out here spyin' for the elf chief, an' Hox's orders are to kill any trespassers.'

I fought with the rope. I'd thought about trying to conjure a flame but my palms were tight against the tree bark and saddlewood is resistant to fire. I struggled to try and turn my hands. The rope tore into my flesh. The pain was severe but I managed to turn one hand round to feel the rope with my palm.

The troll violently swung his axe again and again, and soon there was a low creak as, to my horror, the tree began to tilt forward. Jez screamed. The troll stepped out of the way. My heart juddered against my ribcage and I felt like I was going to be sick. This was it – Jez and I were gonna die in the middle of the Chokewoods, flattened under a couple o' trees with no chance of anyone ever finding us. No. I was a medicine mage. Uncle Crazy Wolf was depending on me, along with Chief Red Feather and the whole of the elf tribe. I closed my eyes and focused my mind, soon feeling my palm grow hotter and hotter.

'Timber!' the troll bellowed, the snake reappearing from underneath his shirt to hiss loudly. 'So long, elf! Best I can do for a tombstone is a great big lump of standard-gauge, iron rail track, and with the wheels of the Flyer shuntin' over your grave, why, your bones'll be shakin' from now till doomsday.' And he laughed gruffly, stepping backwards away from the stricken tree.

As the tree lurched forward, the heat flared in my palm and I felt the ropes slacken around my arms and legs. My heart leaped like a wood frog as, limbs thrashing, I fought for my freedom. The ropes fell away and I dropped with them, landing awkwardly on the forest floor, right in the path of the tree.

The fireball now fully formed in my hand, I scrambled over to Jez just as, with a deafening noise, the enormous saddlewood tree crashed down behind me. I flung the fireball towards the rope that bound Jez to her tree. She was free in seconds and dropped to the ground.

And we ran.

Glancing back I saw the troll who'd tried to kill us, and a few others, were in hot pursuit. 'Spirits alive! We're not out of it yet, the snake-bellies are after us.'

'So now we know Hox was lyin' through those crooked teeth.' Jez panted.

'Yeah, he was lyin', all right. They're Hox's men, illegally clearing the forest for the new rail link to Blackwater.'

We plunged on through the woods, leaping over the twisty roots and ducking under low branches. I hoped the trolls would tire and give up. They certainly didn't look like the fittest bunch of critters on the rock. Then I heard the big troll curse at the others and I glanced back to see they had fallen into a hole in the forest floor, maybe a wolfer pit, and were struggling to crawl out. That left only the big troll but he was gaining ground on us.

'He's getting closer, we've got to run faster,' I panted, knowing full well I was pretty much at top speed. Every step was making my head pound, and at times I thought I might pass out. But then Jez would shout directions, and I didn't argue. There was no right way or wrong way, just an escape-from-the-snake-bellied-troll way.

The troll rasped, 'Get back here, ya little demon snoops, or I'll skin ya alive. I shoulda put my axe through your neck, half-breed, instead o' that tree trunk.'

Jez let out a scream as the troll's axe, destined for my back, whistled past my hat lodging in a tree up ahead. This snake-belly was determined, almost to the extreme.

Around us the trees seemed to become more sparsely packed together and it was getting noticeably lighter. We soon realised why.

'We've come to the edge of the forest,' Jez announced.

I wasn't sure if that was good news or bad. No forest meant no cover from flying axes, and no more trees to lose the troll in, not that we were having much success. And it was because of this that I found myself gasping, 'Keep running!'

Jez stared over at me, blue eyes wild and black hair matted to her sweat-covered face. 'But we'll be sitting ducks.'

'He's gonna catch us no matter what . . . c'mon.'

I didn't have a plan and even if I did I was too short of breath to explain it to Jez. Instead I ran headlong out of the Chokewoods.

I squinted, as the shadowy, dim-lit forest was abruptly drawn back like a pair of curtains to unveil wide blue sky, stretching to the horizon. The ground was much harder after the soft, leafy foliage of the forest floor, and jarring under foot; my head pounded. But an even greater jolt came when I realised that not only was the ground hard, there wasn't very much of it – we'd stumbled out of the forest only to find ourselves on the edge of the eastern arm! And suddenly there was nowhere left to run.

The troll burst out of the woods close behind us,

shielding his eyes from the daylight, yelling that we were dead meat.

I envied Moonshine. The edge of the rock wasn't a barrier to her, just a springboard to another world, the vast wilderness of sky. But to me and Jez it meant certain death. A plunge into the Wastelands. Jez shot me a glance, her face redder than the elf battle face paint.

'I'm not going down without a fight!' she cried, wielding her knife.

'Me neither.'

There wasn't a whole lot of options. What I didn't want was an axe in the back before I even got a chance to stand and fight. The troll was well within throwing distance and I was sure he had me in his sights for first blood.

And then I stumbled.

I couldn't believe it. I'd easily negotiated a mass of twisty chokewood tree roots then, when I hit flatter ground, I practically trip over my own shadow.

'Will!' Jez cried, stopping up ahead.

A heartbeat later the troll was standing over me, his belly snakes pouring from between the buttons of his shirt, hissing and spitting. He paused, saliva dribbling from his huge wart-covered chin, then he laughed triumphantly, raising the axe to deliver a death blow to my neck.

Hearing Jez scream, I felt my whole body tense with cold fear.

But strangely the axe seemed to freeze above the troll's head. I noticed that he was squinting at something beyond me, something on the rock's edge.

A thunderous boom shook the ground, and the troll's face drained of all colour.

I turned round, following his stare and my jaw dropped open. The horned head of a mighty adult thunder dragon rose over the precipice.

Jez shrieked even louder but her cries were drowned out by another deafening roar as the dragon opened its terrifying jaws, revealing dagger-sharp teeth and a huge lolling tongue.

The troll flung his axe at the beast but missed.

I buried my face in my arms, waiting for the scorching flames to incinerate us all at any moment. There was a loud *whoosh*, like the gust of a strong easterly wind, and I felt a rush of searing-hot air waft across my back, scorching my ears and singeing my hair. I heard the troll curse and stomp around, the flap of dragon wings and then the most awful hissing, followed by a yell.

When I looked up I couldn't believe my eyes. The dragon lay still on the rock's edge, staring at me with huge yellow eyes, its wings folded on its back and smoke spiralling from its nostrils. The troll was nowhere to be seen and I wondered if the sheer heat of the dragon's fiery breath had incinerated him, bones and all.

'He forgot to stop rolling,' the dragon remarked, his rich deep voice resounding in my chest.

'H . . . huh?' I stuttered, still numb with fear.

'Trying to put out the flames on his clothes. He rolled over the edge.'

Stunned that this breathtaking creature would address me, I got to my feet slowly. Jez did the same nearby, and, like me, stood trembling.

'You spared us, why?' I asked.

'I spared the troll too,' explained the dragon. 'Barely scorched his slithering belly snakes. He killed himself with his acrobatics trying to smother the flames, sunlight probably dazzling him so he couldn't see the rock's edge.'

And then it dawned on me. I'd seen this thunder dragon before . . . not too long ago. 'It's you, isn't it? The dragon from Phoenix Rise?'

The dragon nodded, and my heart gave a leap.

'We meet again,' he said. 'Maybe the rock isn't as big as some say.'

'How is your daughter?'

'Recovering, thanks to you. The wounds that you tended to so skilfully are healing well.'

Jez's expression grew more and more bewildered and I suddenly realised she couldn't understand a word the dragon was saying so I quickly filled her in. As I did, her frown turned to a smile.

The dragon puffed out a jet of smoke. 'What are you doing so far from your home being chased by trolls?'

'Trying to find out who really destroyed the new fort near Dugtown. My uncle's gonna be hanged for it but he's innocent.'

'And the troll?'

'A railroad worker who didn't like us hanging about the forest asking questions.'

'Don't think he'll be bothering you any more.'

'No,' I agreed. 'Thank you for saving us.'

Jez tugged my sleeve. 'Tell him I'm mighty grateful to him.'

I relayed Jez's message then told him, 'The elves are in great danger. They are going to be driven from their rightful land by settlers. You've helped us to be able to continue our search for the truth.'

The dragon heaved a huge sigh and I felt the heat of his breath rush over me. 'My ancestors had the same problem. My great-grandfather and others like him were pushed from the tops of the West Rock by human hunters, forced instead to nest on the rock's edge, on ledges, and hunt for prey in the West Woods and Wastelands.

I recalled the stories Yenene had told me when I was little.

'What are your names?' the dragon asked.

'I'm Will and this is my good friend Jez. And I remember your daughter told me your name is Thoryn.'

The dragon gave a snort of smoke from his nostrils. 'You saved the life of my daughter Thowra, Will, and I am grateful to you. I can sense your burden for your uncle and I would like to offer my services.'

I stared at the dragon's concerned yellow eyes. 'You'd help us?'

The fearsome horned head nodded. 'I notice you have no horses. Perhaps you need a ride somewhere?'

I told Jez the dragon's name and about his offer to give us a ride. She was just as shocked as I that this great creature would stoop to help us. Jez suggested flying to the place where we'd been blown off the trail. It was a good idea. I turned to Thoryn and swallowed hard. 'We are honoured you would help us. If it is not too much trouble, we'd sure appreciate a ride back to the gorge.'

The dragon
kneeled down on
his front legs and let
us clamber onto his back.

Riding a dragon was a lot harder
than riding Moonshine. There was no saddle,
and I had to cling to one of the spines that ran down the
length of the dragon's neck.

Still, it was an improvement on a few days ago. At
least this time I was up on top of the dragon and not
dangling from its mighty claws.

We took to the sky. I couldn't
believe I was actually riding a dragon.

Jez hollered in my ear. 'Yeeehaaaaa!'

'It's down there, where that gorge widens,' I instructed Thoryn.

'Ah, I feared this is where you spoke of. I'm afraid I can't fly much farther. There are sky rocks around here.'

'Sky rocks? What are they?' Jez asked.

'Great boulders, like the ones that fall from the western arm when it trembles, only much worse. These travel a lot faster and blow outward from the rock's edge. Many dragons have met their deaths being struck by one.'

'We don't want to put you in any danger, Thoryn. Wherever you feel it is safe to land is fine with us.'

Thoryn looked skywards. 'It's beginning to get dark, might be best if we find somewhere safe to spend the night.'

Jez and I agreed and Thoryn brought us safely down in a sheltered area of the gorge near a few scattered tree clumps, with some boulders we could use as chairs.

Jez constructed a ring of stones while I gathered twigs for kindling and a few dead branches. I set the kindling and was about to light it with a magic fire ball when Thoryn breathed a jet of flame, instantly igniting it.

214

I laughed. 'That's sure a whole lot quicker than elf magic.'

Jez fetched more dead wood, and by the time I returned with two fat rabbits and two fewer blowgun darts there was a roaring fire to cook them on.

We shared the meal with Thoryn, though I figured it was kind of too little to fill a fully grown dragon. But he was so appreciative you would've thought we'd served him up a whole cow. And when, later, we curled up near the fire to sleep, Thoryn extended a leathery wing to cover Jez and me, sheltering us from the wind.

CHAPTER TWELVE

★

The Stone-spitter

The next morning Thoryn, in spite of his fear of the deadly sky rocks, flew us to roughly where we'd abandoned our search when the tornado had struck.

Dismounting to examine the terrain, I soon discovered that my worries were confirmed. The tracks had been smoothed over by the swirling winds. My heart dropped into my cowboy boots. We'd lost the only lead we had to go on.

'C'mon, we'll just have to search harder,' Jez cried.

We searched for ages. Thoryn stayed with us to help, trudging along on huge scaly limbs. Now and again, where he felt there was no danger from sky rocks, he'd take to the air, skimming low over the ground in the hope of spotting something.

Finally we picked up the faintest of tracks at the foot of a low hill. We followed the trail towards the edge of the rock when all of a sudden Jez called, 'Look, there's a cave!'

'The tracks seem to lead right up to it,' I gasped. 'Let's go inside.'

'The dark confines of the rock are no place for a creature of the sky,' Thoryn told us. 'I'll wait for you out here.'

'Thank you, Thoryn,' I said. 'We sure appreciate you helping us.'

I found a saddlewood tree and, snapping off a couple of low branches, stripped them of their bark with Jez's knife. I gave one of the branches to her then, taking a deep breath, I led the way into the mouth of the cave – the saddlewood glowed a ghostly purple light, illuminating our path.

'This place is even creepier than the Chokewoods. D'ya think anyone lives here?' Jez asked.

I felt something furry scurry over my feet. 'Dust rats, for one thing.'

'Had my fill o' them, thank you very much,' she commented, referring to the knee-scraping time she'd spent working in Deadrock Tin Mine, crawling through the narrow air vents to keep them clear of dust-rat nests.

I thought I saw something move on the cave wall and remembered the stykes I'd encountered in Deadrock. Stykes are living stalactite-like creatures that cling to dark tunnels and mine roofs waiting for a passing dust rat, or even an unwary resident of Deadrock, so they can drop on them, devouring them with saw-sharp teeth. I raised my saddlewood torch, pulling a gruesome sight from the shadows – a row of enormous skulls lined the cave wall like a display of macabre trophies. The two giant lower canines extending far past the gaping nostril holes told me they were unmistakeably thunder-dragon skulls. A frost-cold tingle shot down my spine and the hairs on my neck stood up. So there *were* folk living here. But who? What sort of folk would do this to one of the most amazing creatures on the whole of the West Rock?

'Just as well Thoryn couldn't come in here,' I said, mesmerised by the grinning skulls.

'Just as well Moonshine didn't come, either,' Jez echoed. 'Look!'

Beyond the skulls a pick-tooth wolf pelt hung

nailed to the wall, its head, tail and limbs splayed out like the points of a sheriff's badge, and, sickeningly, two grey windhorse wings had been carefully hung on both sides of it in a ghastly display. Revulsion and anger welled up within me. I found it impossible to believe anyone could be so cruel.

Jez drew her little bone-handled knife with a shudder. 'Best be on our guard. Those skulls an' skins didn't get up there by themselves, that's for sure.'

We journeyed on, soon entering a large cavern.

'I've heard Uncle Crazy Wolf talk about the hollow hills. Reckon we must be inside one of them.'

Crouching, Jez examined bits of iron equipment that littered the cavern floor. 'What is all this?'

'It's like the stuff you'd see at the iron forge at Oretown.'

A large slab of flat, table-like stone stood in the centre of the cavern and, holding my torch close, I saw that there was something on top of it. At first I thought it was a map scroll, but examining it more closely I realised it was plans for something; a drawing of a long cylindrical object with wheels, and below it numbers and writing – elf writing! It looked interesting and important. Rolling it up I stuffed it into my belt.

'Will, look at this. It's . . . it's incredible!'

Jez waved the saddlewood branch over to a large shadowy object, and the heads of three fearsome, open-mouthed thunder dragons wrought in iron suddenly surged out of the gloom. My heart thumped inside my ribs.

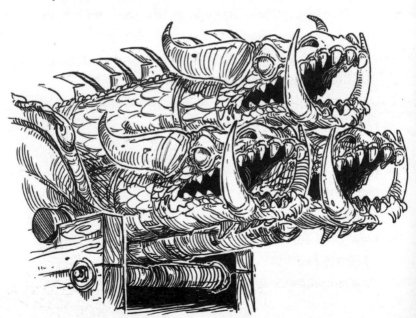

The creatures were chillingly detailed, even down to the dagger-sharp lower canines and cold staring eyes. They decorated the ends of three long cylindrical barrels of iron, crafted together in a triangular shape – two barrels on the bottom and one barrel on top; all of which were fixed to a sturdy wooden base. Whatever it was it looked like it wasn't quite finished two of the four large metal-rimmed wheels lay on their side. It looked similar to the drawings I had stuffed in my belt. A pyramid of boulders sat piled up beside the object.

'Sky rocks,' I breathed.

Jez stared at me. 'What?'

'Look at this pile of boulders here. Do you think these are what Thoryn spoke of?'

'Sky rocks,' she echoed, running her hands over the top boulder. 'They've been specially rounded to make them all the same size. Reckon they could be, right enough, but I reckon something else too.'

'What?'

'Reckon they could be what crashed into the fort!'

I gasped. 'Of course, they're about the right size.'

We both stared at each other in shock until a sickening stink stabbed at my nostrils.

'You smell something, Jez?'

'Yeah, smells like . . .'

'Like dead meat,' came a muffled voice from the gloom. 'Always does in here.'

I froze. 'Who's there?'

'Wolfer . . . with a gun, so unless *you* wanna be dead meat, I'd drop your weapons right now.'

I recognised the voice almost immediately. 'Imelda Hyde!' I breathed, hardly believing the words as they came out.

'Well, if it ain't the wizard spy and his little girlfriend come to get me outta here,' she scoffed. 'Dark spirit sure does work in mysterious ways. Come closer so I can smell me some fresh elf skin and prime dwarf hide.'

We moved slowly towards the grotesque sniffing and snorting noises she began to make. I held out the saddlewood branch illuminating the shadowy figure lying slumped against the far cavern wall. She wore the same filthy rags she'd been wearing in the Trunk and Arms saloon but now her wide-brimmed black hat lay next to her on the ground. I was shocked to see that some of her head bandages had come off, revealing purple scarred skin, tinged with green. And the pointed top of one of her ears was clearly visible among strands of black straggly hair.

'S'far enough,' she croaked, waving the barrel of the gun at Jez. 'And I told yez to drop your weapons.'

Jez dropped the knife, which clattered on the cavern floor, and I tossed down my blowgun but clutched the bag to my side.

As Imelda tried to sit up straighter I noticed her face contort with pain. She cursed, clasping a blood-stained bandaged hand to her leg, and I saw that her coat – which was also spattered with blood – was pocked with bullet holes.

'You've been shot?' I said.

'Course I been shot. You some sort of idiot?' she groaned. 'And I'd be dead and gone if it weren't for this piece of hide I got tailored to my belly.'

'Hide don't stop a bullet,' Jez remarked.

'Adult thunder-dragon hide does,' she hissed through gritted yellow teeth.

'What's going on?' I asked. 'And what is this creepy place?'

'Water.' She swallowed hard. 'You got water in that bag, an' food?'

I handed her the container of water and a dried beef strip, and she took a long gulp of water then devoured the meat, tearing hungrily at it like some wild animal, like a pick-tooth wolf, her ghastly broken teeth flashing in the saddlewood light. When she'd finished she said, 'This *creepy* place as you call it is *my* place – where I skin me some pelts, hunt me some dragons and build me some weapons.'

'Like this weapon?' Jez paced to the middle of the cavern, her torch illuminating the fearsome heads of the wrought-iron thunder dragons.

'I call them stone-spitters; crafted them with my own bare hands. They're more destructive than the fiercest tornado and more powerful than a rock quake.'

Jez scowled at her. 'Powerful enough to shoot a thunder dragon from the sky?'

'Now you're getting the picture!' Imelda grinned. 'Dragons fly real close to the rock out here.'

'Hunting thunder dragons is illegal, orders of the high sheriff,' I spat.

'Not in Imelda Hyde's book, it ain't.' She winced

224

and grabbed her leg. 'As to your first question, what's goin' on? Well, I've been a cursed fool, that's what, thinkin' I could trust those two waste o' skin Gatlans.'

'The Gatlans were here?' I gasped, though I figured it made sense. Last time I'd seen Imelda she'd been plotting with the Gatlans at the meeting in the saloon. But what had they been plotting?

'Must be a couple o' days ago now since they pulled their double-crossin' guns on me. There was a shoot-out endin' with me takin' too many hits, fallin' over and knockin' myself out on a jagged rock. The low-bellies didn't wanna pay up for the stone-spitter, either that or they figured on keepin' as few folk as possible involved in their evil plan.' Her face reddened and she clenched her bandaged fists. 'Not that they'd have even had a plan if it weren't for me. The whole thing was my idea. From the night of the rancher's meeting in the saloon when I told them I had a secret weapon that could destroy the new fort, mimickin' an elf-mage thunderball so they could pin the blame on the elves.'

'So it was a weapon like this that destroyed the fort?' I said.

'Bigger,' she replied. 'Fires six boulders at a time.

This is the first one I built – only fires three boulders.'

I gasped. 'I can't believe you'd betray your own people.'

She peered at me, slit-eyed through her dirty face bandages. 'How could you know that, kid?'

'My uncle Crazy Wolf told me. He's the medicine mage of Gung-Choux Village. At one time you were apprenticed under him. He told me you showed a lot of promise, if only you hadn't turned to the dark side.'

'Crazy Wolf!' she spat, her voice laced with venom. 'You tellin' me that stupid ol' wizard's your uncle?'

'He's far from stupid. You should've listened to him, then you might not be in the mess you're in today.'

'Crazy Wolf turned his back on me just cos I wanted to do things a bit different, experiment a bit. And, as for betrayin' my own people, the elf folk stopped bein' *my people* a long time ago when they threw me outta Gung-Choux Village.'

'Medicine magic is a force for good, you were using it for evil.'

'What would you know about it, kid? You're talkin' about medicine magic like you're some kinda expert . . .Wait a minute.' She paused peering at me with those dark probing eyes. 'Now I get it. Crazy Wolf has been teachin' *you* medicine magic, hasn't he?'

I nodded slowly.

'Now this is gettin' interestin', and would explain your little trick shootin' that arrow through my hat back on the western arm. Keep talkin', kid. How much do you know?'

'A bit.'

I noticed her gaze hop between me and her leg wound. 'He been teachin' you 'bout healin'?'

'No,' I fibbed. Maybe I was talking too much? She was poking me for information and I was playing right into her hands. I felt like stuff was happening too fast. I had to keep focused. I had to figure a way of getting out of here to pass on my new-found knowledge to the high sheriff and free my uncle from Mid-Rock jail.

'Yer lyin', kid. He's bound to have. That's the first thing they train you in when you're learnin' medicine magic – most of the other principles all follow on from it. Toss me that bag you been clutchin' tighter than new boots.'

'My bag, but why? There's nothing in it but blowgun darts and a few dried beef strips.'

She pulled back the trigger on her gun, pointing it directly at me. 'The bag!'

I set it by her side. As I did she seized me by the wrist, her long, sharp nails cutting deep into my flesh. Her bandaged face was barely inches from mine and I could smell her rancid breath. 'Don't ever talk back to me, kid. Y'hear?' she fumed.

The pain was excruciating, it felt like my arm was on fire, but I stifled the cry in my throat and gritting my teeth I nodded. She let go, and I backed up, staring at the little semicircles of blood starting to form on my skin.

Rummaging inside she fished out the little beaded pouch stuffed with magical dried herbs.

'Just a few beef strips, huh?' she rasped. 'Hope you're a better healer than you are a liar. If I'm not mistaken these herbs are gonna buy me a brand-new leg.' She tossed me the pouch. 'I've long since forgotten all that magic stuff, kid, so I'm gonna let you do it.

Do a good job and maybe I'll let you both walk outta here with skin on your bones.'

I glanced at Jez, her fearful expression telling me she felt just as trapped as I did. 'Talk's cheap' was a favourite saying of my pa's when he'd been alive. Would Hyde really let us go if I healed her? Or would she shoot us anyway? Either way I didn't really have much of a choice.

Stomach churning from the smell of her filthy clothes, I moved closer, crouching next to Imelda's wounded leg. When I informed her I'd need to cut her trouser she just nodded and grunted. Jez handed me her knife and I cut the material, exposing the gun-shot wounds. Clotted blood adorned much of the injuries, which was the only reason she was still alive otherwise she'd have bled to death, though I did spot an old piece of rope she'd probably used as a tourniquet. The bullet had most likely shattered the bone.

Carefully I sprinkled the healing herbs on the wounds, exactly the way Uncle Crazy Wolf had shown me. I focused my mind, my outstretched palms hovering over the leg, then I began to chant the magic words in the ancient elf language.

I could feel Imelda's cold staring eyes watching me like a wood hawk but she said nothing. Maybe she remembered from her own mage training that healing magic is best conjured in silence.

I laid my hands on the wound and Imelda flinched slightly, grunting. The dried herbs moistened, growing warm beneath my tingling fingers, and I finished the magic words.

'That's it,' I announced. 'Though I've never healed a broken bone before so I . . .'

Imelda jerked her leg up, bending it at the knee to examine the wounds. 'Demons alive, kid, you did it – it worked. I can feel it. Ha!' She got to her feet. 'You're good, kid. Y'know, I'd have stuck at all this magic stuff if your crazy uncle hadn't burned all my dark-magic books.'

Dusting herself down she grabbed my bag with the blowgun shoved inside it. 'Got me my leg back, now to get my property back. Where are your horses tied up? The Gatlans helped themselves to my windhorse.'

'We ain't got horses,' said Jez.

'Quit lyin' to me, you gotta have horses. How'd you get out here?'

'On foot,' I said. I hoped Thoryn had flown back to

his den. I didn't want him to get caught up in all this.

'We'll see about that, won't we? Let's go.' And she marched us at gunpoint out of the cave, moving briskly on her newly healed leg.

Outside I blinked in the bright sunlight then my heart sank. Thoryn lay sprawled out like a small hill near the cave entrance, his scaly back slowly rising and falling as he slept.

'What in blazes – a dragon!' Instinctively Imelda raised her gun.

'No, don't shoot!' I cried. 'Look, OK, we started out on foot then we met a dragon and he flew us here. His name is Thoryn.'

'A cowboy who can do magic an' ride thunder dragons, eh?' Imelda sneered. 'Why you're just full o' surprises, kid.' She lowered the weapon. 'Been a waste of a bullet anyway, adult dragon skin is bullet proof.'

Instead Imelda grabbed Jez, shoving the barrel of her gun into her back. 'OK, here's the deal, though I never thought I'd hear myself say this. You're gonna wake up your scaly friend here and tell him we're hitchin' a ride inland to the Gatlans' place. But I warn you, try anythin' and I'll have a gun wedged between your little girlfriend's shoulder blades, you got it?'

'But what if he refuses? Dragons are wary of flying too far inland.'

I noticed Thoryn was already beginning to stir, a plume of smoke rising from his great nostrils as he opened a huge green eye.

'Just make sure he doesn't,' Imelda hissed. 'For both your sakes.'

CHAPTER THIRTEEN

★

Dragon Ride

The sun shrank lower in the sky as Imelda, Jez and I flew inland.

Thoryn, while wary of the foul-smelling stranger on his back, had nonetheless agreed to take us on one final flight to the Gatlans' ranch, though if he'd known one of his passengers hunted and killed thunder dragons he'd probably have incinerated the whole lot of us. I explained to the dragon that the Gatlans were the evil ranchers behind the conspiracy to drive the elf folk from their rightful land and he listened attentively.

'Thoryn, you have been more than a help to us,' I told him as we flew. 'And I take none of your kindness for granted. I hope I haven't overstepped the mark by asking for this final favour.'

'Nonsense, friends, I can't say I am not uneasy about flying over land but nevertheless I feel it is worth the risk if it helps you to right a great wrong.'

I rode up front with Jez behind me. Imelda brought up the rear, the barrel of her gun prodding into Jez's backbone. I was fearful for our safety and rode with a stone lump in my throat. Imelda was pretty crazy, and I was sure if she was intent on killing the Gatlans then she'd have no hesitation in shooting both of us if we didn't take her where she wanted to go.

'Heck, never thought I'd see the day when I rode on the back of a real live thunder dragon!' Imelda cried as we soared higher. 'I'm impressed too, kid, you're steerin' him like a windhorse.'

As we flew over Dugtown I spotted something that made me curious – the Flyer had been halted at Dugtown station. There was no steam spewing from its stack so it wasn't going anywhere. It seemed kind of strange. Stranger still was why there were sky-cavalry soldiers clustered around the old steamer, on the platform like they were guarding it. What was going on? I eyed the last freight carriage – the one Jez and I couldn't get open. Was the stone-spitter inside?

We flew onwards to where the land spread out in every direction, flat, dry and dusty. Rail track snaked its way from Dugtown in the east towards Gung-Choux Village and the settled lands.

'Head west please, mighty Thoryn, following the rail track.'

He responded immediately, manoeuvring on majestic wings, soaring faster.

It was then I heard the faint sound of elf drums carried on the wind. But the rhythm was quite different, more urgent, a fast-paced *Thud! Thud! Thud!* These were not the war drum beats I'd heard days ago. No. Things had gotten worse.

'Battle drums!' I breathed.

We flew a little farther, following the winding rail track, and the sight that greeted us from the air made my blood run frost-cold.

In the open prairie between the settled lands and Gung-Choux Village, at the foot of some low hills, the battle lines had been drawn. Two armies faced each other.

On one side was a rank of more than a hundred sky-cavalry troops on horseback, dressed in battle uniform of blue and yellow, their sabres and long-barrelled pistols flashing in the sun. In the middle of the front line of troops, astride a beautiful white mount, I saw the high sheriff, Septimus Flynt, barking orders at his men. Then, further back, tucked in behind the cavalry, a very different band of troops had gathered – the Gatlans' sordid little army of a few-dozen men on ranch horses who, compared to the smart cavalry, looked colourless and bedraggled, dressed in dirty ranchers' clothes.

Opposing them, across the prairie, some distance from the outskirts of Gung-Choux Village, stood an army of elf braves. The front line consisted of a row of face-painted warriors wielding pointed spears and holding round, painted shields, which they had locked together in a defensive shield-wall. Then there were several lines of archers, bows and arrows at the ready. At the centre of the archers, holding aloft a battle standard, stood Chief Red Feather, wearing a plumed battle headdress. Lastly, behind all these, I could just about make out the muscular elf drummer – the beating heart of the elf army – pounding the war drums. *Thud! Thud! Thud!*

I remembered my uncle telling me that the medicine mage's battle position was at the centre of the front

line behind the shield-wall so that all the other braves could see him and he could freely wield his power at the enemy. But there was no mage in this army, and it was my fault.

Tears welled in my eyes. 'We're too late, the battle is about to begin and without my uncle's presence and power, the elves will be massacred!' I blamed myself. A poor excuse of a medicine mage I'd been for my uncle. I hadn't acted quickly enough.

Jez put a hand on my shoulder. 'Ain't started yet, Will, so we ain't too late.'

Imelda roared with laughter. 'Wow, now that's something else. The high sheriff don't hang around. Must be real mad, thinkin' the elves smashed up his precious fort. I hate to admit it but the Gatlans done a pretty good job gettin' the sky cavalry on their side so quickly.'

Jez pointed to the dishevelled army of ranchers. 'There's Buck Gatlan mounted on a black stallion, I recognise him from the gunsmith's shop.'

They were both there – Buck and Whip – tucked in behind the cavalry. Even in battle they were cowards, riding behind the front cavalry rank so they wouldn't have to take the full force of the elf spears.

'Demons alive!' Imelda squealed. 'If it ain't the murderin' brothers themselves. Well they're in for one heck of a shock when they see ol' Imelda's risen from the dead. Get me down there, kid, and make it quick. I can't wait to put a great big slug of a bullet in both their ugly grinnin' faces.'

'Thoryn, are you OK to go on?' I asked, conscious that the thunder dragon was getting mixed up in something that was nothing to do with him, yet he offered no complaint.

'Yes,' he said. 'It is not good to see rock folk square up to one another in battle like this. If I can help then I will stay with you.'

I flew Thoryn lower and, as I did so, the hate-filled eyes of the soldiers and braves on the ground were gradually drawn away from each other towards Thoryn's descending shadow. The lines of elf braves recoiled in awe, and cavalry horses stirred, whinnying loudly and nervously pawing the ground with their hooves at the sight of the mighty winged beast.

I brought Thoryn down close to where the Gatlan army stood bunched in a group on the sky cavalry's right flank. The high sheriff, recognising Jez and me, galloped over with two officers, his jaw gaping open in disbelief. They pulled up their nervous-looking horses as close as they dared to the dragon.

'You needn't fear the dragon, he is a friend. His name is Thoryn.'

I paused, though I was bursting to tell him about the stone-spitter and show him the plans I had stuffed in my belt but Imelda raised the bandaged hand in a gesture of peace. Her other hand still held a gun to Jez's back.

'I got no quarrel with you or your men, high sheriff,' she cried. 'But there's certain o' your company here, name o' Gatlan, stole my property then tried to kill me, an' that's what I got issue with.' She glowered at Buck and Whip who stood frozen to the spot, staring at Imelda. I was sure I noticed Buck's trigger finger twitching madly.

'Who are you?' the high sheriff quizzed.

'Name's Imelda Hyde, a wolfer.'

'You gonna let some crazy wolfer interrupt this here battle, sir?' Buck spat. 'We stole nothing from her. I've never set eyes on her in my life.'

Suddenly Jez, in a lightning-quick move, slid off Thoryn's back onto the ground. In a moment of mad bravery she ran towards the high sheriff crying, 'Imelda is a hunter, but not just wolves – she hunts thunder dragons. She forges weapons like you never saw before . . .'

'Cursed dwarf!' Imelda screamed drawing her gun.

Twisting round, I managed to grab her arm just as she pulled the trigger. There was deafening bang but the bullet whistled harmlessly skywards. Angrily I shoved her bandaged wrist down hard on a spiky scale, and she dropped the gun, shrieking with pain.

Jez kept yelling. 'She made a weapon called a stone-spitter – fires boulders the size o' watermelons, the Gatlans stole it and used it on the fort. They had it all planned to make it look like the medicine mage did it and to turn the sky cavalry against the elves!'

The high sheriff's face drained of colour. His gaze darted between the Gatlans, Jez, Imelda and me, 'What are you talking about? Is this true?'

'Yes, it's true, sir,' I added. 'We saw a smaller version of the weapon back at the Hollow Hills.'

On hearing this Whip – his face like thunder – galloped forward, wielding his six-shot blaster gun. He shot off two rounds at Imelda and me. He missed, but

Thoryn seemed to take the attack personally and reared up like a giant clattersnake spewing a jet of red-hot flame at Whip. The rancher's winged stallion had only seconds to react, leaping into the air to climb high over our heads as Whip's six-shot cracked again.

Imelda cried, 'Do something, kid. Crazy Gatlan's gonna kill us both!'

Thoryn didn't need to be spurred by me, in a heartbeat he extended his wings and took to the sky.

Strangely, amidst all the pandemonium, I was sure I saw Buck fly off too, though in the opposite direction, away from the battle scene towards Dugtown.

Whip's horse circled the less-agile thunder dragon as the crack of a six-shot rang in my ears. Imelda now wielded a pistol. Being a weapons freak she probably had a whole stash hidden in her coat, but she couldn't get a clear shot as Whip's horse swooped, climbed and turned, chasing around the dragon. Thoryn instinctively would not want to harm the innocent horse, although the scowl on Whip's black mount was almost as hate-filled as that of its rider.

Then Whip's six-shot ran out of bullets and he fumbled for his rifle, allowing us precious time to swoop in closer. Thoryn soared over the top, the down draft of his huge wing beats nearly knocking Whip's horse from the sky – but not before his dagger-sharp talons plucked Whip, still clutching his rifle, by the back of his coat from the saddle. Thrashing about like a gutfish on the end of a fishing line Whip fired the rifle pointlessly into Thoryn's bullet-proof underbelly, only making him angrier.

Whip whistled for his horse to fly to him, yelling, 'Let me go, ya scaly freak!'

Thoryn did as he was told. Sort of.

Tossing the cowboy up into the sky, he incinerated him in a searing hot jet of flame. Whip turned into what looked like a lump of black charcoal falling from the sky, breaking up into small pieces that were carried away on the wind.

'Nice work!' cried Imelda. 'Y'know, I could get to like thunder dragons.'

Thoryn landed not far from the sky cavalry as Imelda cried, 'Where's the other one?'

And that's when I felt it, a stomach-wrenching tremor of the sort I'd only ever felt on the western arm. The horses felt it too and pawed the ground anxiously. Soldiers stared at each other. The sky darkened. My gut instinct told me something was wrong – very wrong. To feel such a strong tremor this far east was unheard of. It could only mean there'd been a significant tremor on the western arm. I thought about Yenene – I couldn't bear it if anything happened to her. But then, moments later, the ground was still once more and the rumble of quaking rock was suddenly replaced by another familiar sound – that of a steam engine.

There was a loud whistle then a gunshot, and I turned round to see the Flyer steaming along the plains. Last time I'd seen the old steamer it had been at Dugtown station and I now realised why all the soldiers had been gathered around it. They'd stopped it for safety reasons, knowing that battle was about to commence very near the rail route to protect any passengers who might be aboard from getting caught up in the fighting. The Flyer now screeched to a halt. A single gunshot sounded from the front of the train and a man fell from the driver's cab onto the ground to lie motionless. Was it the driver? And who'd shot him? A hatted figure jumped from the cab, running the length of the train to open the last freight carriage. It was Buck. Pulling back the doors he clambered inside the carriage, laughing manically.

With a low rumble the heads of six, open-mouthed, metal thunder dragons slowly emerged from the gloomy carriage. Buck edged the fearsome weapon forward with its long cylindrical barrels of iron stacked together in a triangular shape and fixed onto a sturdy wooden cart.

'Hey, wolfer, you want your stone-spitter – you're gonna have to come an' get it!' Buck yelled.

I stared, scarcely able to believe my eyes. So the stone-spitter *had* been inside that locked freight carriage Jez and I had examined at Mid-Rock station. And it had been coupled to the train ever since; the Gatlans hadn't even bothered to move it to a goods yard in the station.

'That's it, that's the weapon that destroyed the fort!' I yelled to the high sheriff.

He gasped. 'Then it's true. The elf folk are completely innocent in all this, as is your uncle Crazy Wolf.' He addressed the soldier to his left. 'Captain, send a herald at once to Chief Red Feather saying we seek urgent counsel with him then get your men down there and arrest Buck Gatlan immediately!'

The captain began rallying the sky cavalry to ride down to the train.

'Danged son of a marsh toad's got my weapon.

Get after him, kid!' screamed Imelda. We had to stop Buck from firing the weapon. I spurred Thoryn to take flight once more and we chased, ahead of the cavalry, towards the Flyer.

As we rode closer, though, Buck fired the stone-spitter. There was a sky-shattering boom as, with a great cloud of billowing smoke, six stone projectiles were propelled towards us like enormous speeding bullets. One of the boulders struck Thoryn on the wing and he fell, tumbling from the sky, throwing Imelda from his back. Using every last ounce of strength I only just managed to cling on and, before Thoryn ploughed into the ground, I leaped clear of the stricken dragon, rolling across the dusty ground. Miraculously I escaped with a few bruises. Imelda wasn't so lucky; I saw her sprawled nearby, not moving. I took my bag, with my blowgun inside it, from her lifeless body.

Buck hooted and danced like a demented rock hyena. Hurriedly he tipped more stone bullets into the dragon-carved barrel ends of the stone-spitter.

'Shoulda fired a boulder at her wolfer belly back at the hollow hills.' Buck was roaring. 'Still, guess that means this iron baby's all mine now.'

Examining Thoryn I was relieved to find he was still breathing, though I couldn't risk stopping to help him now.

Getting to my feet I looked back towards the sky cavalrymen. Some unseated soldiers were chasing after their fleeing horses, others tried to steer their mounts back into formation, but the horses had been badly frightened by the thunderous weapon and seemed almost uncontrollable. Someone had to stop Buck and that someone was me. But what could I do? All I had was my blowgun and some frog poison. Then I spotted something glinting in the sunlight – Imelda's gun. Without hesitation I picked it up and stuffed it in my belt.

'Never thought I'd see sky-cavalry horses galloping away like spooked steers!' said a voice behind me.

I turned round to see a pale white horse alight on the dusty ground. 'Shy! Where'd you come from?'

'Elf battle lines,' she explained. 'Chief Red Feather says he knew you'd come; that the Great Spirit has sent you to save us. Some of the elf braves are coming to help the sky cavalry.'

'Where's Jez?'

'She's back at the elf lines with Tyrone. He rode Jez's horse over from the ranch. C'mon, climb on and I'll get you down to that carriage.'

As I mounted Shy I saw the high sheriff stride forward with a group of sky-cavalrymen on older-looking horses that hadn't been too spooked by the stone-spitter. 'Buck Gatlan, you're charged with high treason against the sky cavalry and the West Rock, the murder of the sky-cavalry guards and the destruction of cavalry property.'

'Y'know, I've just had me a thought,' Buck shouted back. 'What gives you authority over the whole rock, anyway? Seems to me the eastern arm would be governed just fine if it was allowed to be ruled by its own people, maybe even have its *own* high sheriff. Give you more time to manage the affairs of Mid-Rock and keep your beak out of *our* business.'

'You'd like that, wouldn't you, Buck? And let me guess who you'd suggest for high sheriff of the eastern arm – Buck Gatlan, am I right?'

'Catch on mighty quick, Flynt.' He grinned, rolling another boulder into the end of the weapon. 'Can't see too many opposing me on account of me now havin' a bigger gun than pretty much anybody else around. And that makes me the most powerful person on the rock.'

'Takes more than a gun to make a sheriff. Your brother's dead, Buck – incinerated by the thunder dragon during an aerial gun battle. He died needlessly. Don't be a fool, give yourself up!'

News of his brother's death seemed to incense Buck even more and he thrust a final boulder down the iron dragon's gaping mouth.

A few of the soldiers riding with the high sheriff aimed their rifles, along with some elf archers on foot who raised their bows, but he waved them down. 'Wait. Hold your fire, there are innocent men, women and children aboard that train. We need to get closer.'

Sure enough frightened passengers were alighting from the train to flee for safety behind the elf battle lines into Gung-Choux Village.

The high sheriff rode closer, followed by his cavalry and a band of elf archers, but suddenly their luck ran out. The stone-spitter roared again, and several boulders crashed into the brave soldiers, splintering men and horses. I heard one of the boulders whistle over my head.

'That was too close!' I gasped. 'C'mon, Shy, it's up to us. We've got to do something, and quick. Let's get down there while Buck reloads the stone-spitter.'

Moonshine took to the sky and, like a speeding bullet, flew to the carriage Buck was inside.

The rancher cursed at me and shot off a couple of rounds but he missed.

'You're dead meat, wizard spy. An' I blame you for all this.'

I landed Shy as close as I dared to the train. 'Listen, Shy. I want you to fly back to Jez. It's too dangerous, I can take it from here.'

'What are you gonna do?'

Buck fired again, jumping out of the carriage. But then his gun clicked empty and he fiddled, taking bullets out of his belt.

'Go on, Shy! I'll catch up with you soon.'

Moonshine took to the sky and I strode towards Buck pointing the gun at him.

'Give it up, Buck, or I'll shoot.'

He glowered at me. 'You ain't gonna shoot anybody, kid. I'll be the one doin' the shootin'. If it weren't for you showin' up on the back o' that cursed

252

thunder dragon my brother would still be alive.'

I aimed at his feet then pulled the trigger. *Click!* Empty! And worse, Buck had reloaded and now pointed his gun at me, only he wasn't aiming at my feet. I dived into the driver's cab of the locomotive to escape the bullets. Hearing Buck lurch towards me, I glanced frantically around the cab. An array of pipes, clocks, gauges, wheels and iron levers adorned the front of the engine and I gasped. I could hear Buck muttering and cursing as he stomped after me. What did I think I could do? I'd never been in the engine room of a steam train in my life. I had no idea what all these wheels and levers did. Eyes darting between a few of the longer levers, I pulled back the biggest one. With a jolt the train began to roll forward on the track, gathering speed. Buck jumped onto the footplate and swung the barrel of the six-shot towards me. He had me cornered. I was sure I was a gonner this time.

'You're just like your stupid wizard uncle, boy. If you hadn't stuck your nose into things we could be dividin' up the elf land into ranches. You'd have done all right out of it, but you're too dumb to latch on to a good thing when you see it.'

253

'What's good 'bout stripping elf folk of their rightful land?'

'This rock belongs to no one, 'cept them with the guts to fight for it.'

'Don't take much guts to hide behind the sky cavalry, Buck Gatlan.' I'd been bursting to say it but still couldn't believe it when I did. Buck went purple with anger.

'Why, you smart mouthed yella belly, you're no better than your goody goody deputy-sheriff pa.'

'My pa was worth a hundred o' you.' I felt the elf magic burn in my trembling hands. They would be red-hot and I wanted to reach out and plant my palms on that sneer he wore on his fat face, but I fought it back. I had a terrible feeling of the dark welling up inside me and I wasn't sure I could control it. Was this what had consumed Imelda years ago when she'd been lured into practising dark magic? My uncle said that the mark of a true mage was learning how to have power over the darker side, smothering this anger and instead channelling it for good.

Buck raised his pistol just seconds before the Flyer plunged into the Mid-Rock tunnel and everything went black.

CHAPTER FOURTEEN
★
Crumbling Rock

I froze, feeling my heart gallop inside my chest. I couldn't see a thing. I heard Buck lumber towards me. Then I felt a massive hand pin me by the neck against the wall of the driver's cab, choking the life from me. I could smell his warm breath which stank of bacca weed as he began to laugh in my face.

He pressed the cold barrel of the gun into my forehead. 'Say your prayers, half-breed. I warned you at the gunsmith's that I'd kill you!'

I fought for breath and my head swam. This was it. My luck had finally run out. But suddenly there was another huge tremor, even stronger than the last one. The Flyer jerked madly on the track and Buck was hurled across the cab, cursing loudly. I sucked in a big lungful of air.

A heartbeat later I was on my feet and fumbling out the other side of the train cab, clambering onto a ladder and then beyond it to where I could feel a ledge running along the coal cart. There was a good chance the ledge ran all the way to the first-class carriage. Maybe if I could just get there I'd have time to figure out my next move. Jumping from the train would be crazy – there was no soft tangleweed in the dark tunnel to land on and the fall would probably kill me. Carefully I edged across it. Below me the wheels roared in the darkness, while behind me the rocky tunnel whisked by, dangerously close.

'Where are ya, half-breed?' I heard Buck yell as he banged around the cab.

It didn't take him long to figure out what I'd done.

'Think you're clever, don't ya?' he spat. I heard him follow me out onto the ledge of the coal cart.

Reaching the end of the wagon I blind-jumped the coupling, only just managing to grab the metal railing on the front of the boarding platform, and moments later I was travelling first class for the first time in my

life. But I'd no time to enjoy my new-found status –
normally in first class you don't have a mad, pistol-
waving rancher chasing after you. Buck was hollering
that he was coming to get me. I needed a plan. I needed
a flash of inspiration.

I got one.

To my surprise a flame appeared in the gloom up
ahead. I saw hands, old wrinkled hands, then a face –
the elf conductor.

'Will, it's me. Are you all right?' His bushy eyebrows
leaped up his forehead.

'Yes, I'm OK, but what are you doing here?'

'Is everyone off the train?' he asked.

'Think so.'

'So they kept the weapon on board all the time.'

'It's called a stone-spitter, the Gatlans stole it off a
mad wolfer from the Hollow Hills. Buck's on board too,
he's coming after me. He'll be here any second.'

'I got a feeling Buck Gatlan mightn't be the only
problem we got. The whole rock sounds like it's just
about ready to split apart. Never felt the quakes as bad
as this in the tunnel here.'

The elf conductor extinguished the palm flame

as we both clung to our seats to avoid being thrown across the carriage by the force of the juddering carriage. I wondered if Buck had been thrown from the coal cart.

The Flyer wheels screamed, barely clinging to the track, which shook below them, while outside the window the darkness was illuminated by showers of sparks.

Then a loud gunshot rang out.

'Come on, you little rat, I know you're hiding in here!' Buck yelled, still very much alive and hungry for my blood.

Bullets ricocheted around the carriage and I ducked.

If Buck kept firing randomly the conductor and I would both be dead meat in no time.

I fumbled for my bag. I needed to shoot a poison dart and I couldn't afford to miss.

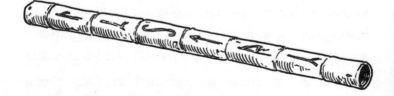

Aiming the blowgun in the darkness, I focused my mind, reaching out with my senses till before me an image of the big rancher, nothing more than a shadow, formed in my mind's eye. But a shadow was good enough for me and I blew sharply into the blowgun. I quickly reloaded and sent another one in the same direction. I heard him curse.

'What the . . .?' And he fired his pistol again.

'Shooting arrows at me, you little worm?'

Next thing there was a thunderous roar and the sound of splitting rock. The whole tunnel shook violently and the Flyer's wheels gave up their struggle to cling onto the fracturing track. The train derailed, careering into the side of the narrow tunnel wall.

I fell to the floor, covering my head with my arms.

The noise was terrible: the scraping of metal on rock, the clang of snapping couplings, the squealing of the wheels as they buckled on the craggy tunnel floor, the splintering of shattered windows showering the interior with glass. The momentum of the train carried it far, groaning and scraping to a halt as daylight filled the carriage. We'd come to a standstill at the end of the tunnel.

'Let's get outta here!' I called, helping the elf conductor to his feet. We stepped over Buck who lay unconscious on the floor. I couldn't be sure if it was from the frog poison or from a blow to the head as the train had derailed.

Opening the front door of the carriage, I blinked in the sunlight, then my heart almost leaped out of my throat.

Where I'd expected to see the coal cart, damaged and with probably most of its load shed, there was nothing. Worse still there was no engine, either. Then, to my horror, I saw the reason why. There was no bridge. The bridge that connected the Mid-Rock to the western arm – that Jez and I had flown past only days earlier when visiting Yenene – had collapsed and fallen into the gorge under the relentless stress of the quakes. The first-class carriage we were aboard had detached from the carriage behind it and come to a halt, balanced precariously on the rock's edge – halfway out the mouth of the tunnel. I stared, trembling almost as violently as the whole of the western arm – great chunks of which were breaking off in front of my eyes like some terrifying stone waterfall. The beating heart of the Flyer was down there too, smashed into a hundred pieces; its great boiler spluttering its last gasps of steam as it was slowly buried under the falling rock.

The western arm was breaking off. And I had to rescue Grandma before it was too late.

'Spirit help us!' gasped the elf conductor standing at my shoulder. 'What are we to do?'

'My grandma's on top of what's left o' that rock and I have to try an' save her.'

'She's what?' the elf conductor baulked. 'Y'mean she never left after the evacuation order?'

I shook my head frantically.

'She refused to believe it was gonna collapse.' I breathed a deep sigh.

Suddenly, with a loud creak, the carriage dipped slightly downwards into the gorge, like the seesaw Pa had made me when I was a kid. My stomach churned as the conductor and I grasped the rail in fear. We didn't dare breathe. I stared into the abyss, realising that one more dip was likely to plunge us both to our deaths. And I was numb with fear.

Looking back I saw a slumbering Buck start to slide towards us, and as he did his weight made the carriage tilt even more. It looked like Buck might kill us all without even knowing it.

'We're not getting out this way, that's for sure, c'mon let's try the other end past Buck before it's too late.'

We were about to make our way past the rancher when the carriage suddenly lurched again and, as it did so, Buck opened one eye. He was awake and breathing. I'd made the mistake of not putting enough frog poison on the dart.

He was also blocking our only escape route. Slowly he got to his feet. I saw he was unarmed and figured his gun had slipped from his hand with the force of the train derailing.

'Move back, Buck!' I yelled. 'The bridge has collapsed; the carriage is balancing on the edge – you're gonna make it tip over!'

'No half-breed kid tells a Gatlan what to do,' he spat. 'Not when I gotta give you back this dart, here, through your thick skull.'

The elf conductor pointed at the sky. 'Will, look!'

'What is it?'

'Horses, two of them. Some friends o' yours, I believe.'

'It's Shy! I don't believe it,' I gasped, breathing a huge sigh of relief. 'And Jez, riding her own horse. They must've flown round the rock after us.'

My gaze darting between Buck, who staggered unsteadily from the effects of the poison, and the windhorses, who flew closer, I made a decision.

'Jez will rescue you,' I told the elf conductor. 'Just be ready to climb on her horse when she flies close. Tell Shy to circle for me, I'll be back.'

'Where are you going?'

'To buy us some time!' I yelled, charging along the carriage aisle to head-butt Buck in the middle of his fat gut. Winded, he fell back, me on top of him, and crashed onto the floor. I felt the carriage steadying, tilting to a more horizontal position.

Behind me I heard Jez yell at the elf conductor to get on her horse and then she called, 'Will, c'mon, you have to get outta there.'

'Fly to Phoenix Creek, I'll see you there. Go!'

I turned back, only to feel Buck's fist slam into my face.

It felt like I'd just flown Shy into the side of the rock. I landed a few feet away, surprised I was still conscious and then wishing I wasn't as the pain seared into my bloodied nose. I waited to feel the next blow, the sole of a cowboy boot on my throat, the butt of a gun around my chin. But nothing happened. Where was he? Then I heard the sound of boots stomping off down the carriage.

'So long, kid, you can fall into the gorge with this ol' rust bucket of a steamer. He paused at the door, a sick grin on his face, then stepped off the back of the carriage into the tunnel. And, with a groan, the carriage pitched rapidly downwards. Arching my neck to stare out the front door I saw that the first-class carriage was on the verge of hurtling into the gorge to join the coal cart and the engine.

But I wasn't ready to join it just yet. I had to find a way out of there for Yenene's sake.

I scrabbled on my hands and knees along the aisle as the carriage began to slide off the edge of the rock. It was nearly vertical as I made it to the back door (the door Buck had used to exit the stricken carriage) and hurled myself at the rail that skirted boarding steps just outside the door. I saw Buck staring at me from the safety of the tunnel floor, waving.

'So long, half-breed. Enjoy the trip. Looks like this ol' tin can's gonna live up to its name – the Flyer!' And he burst into insane laughter.

With a terrible *clang* the carriage slid off the edge of the rock. My heart hammered like an elf war drum and I felt sick.

Suddenly, out of the corner of my eye, I glimpsed something shiny, metal glinting brightly in the sun – the new rail track. Was it close enough? I weighed it up; the carriage was tilting slightly as it slid down to its rocky grave, maybe there was a chance. Maybe if I could just . . . jump.

I leaped off the plummeting rail cart and flew through the air, arms flailing, I got the fingertips of one hand and whole fingers of my other hand onto a piece of the track.

Gasping I swung there, watching the first-class carriage tumble, breaking up as it did, headlong into the gorge, great chunks of metal splintering off it as it careered into jagged outcrops of rock.

'Will, hang on, I'm coming!' called a familiar voice. It was Moonshine soaring out of the sun.

'Good for you, Shy. I can't hold on much longer.'

Moonshine swooped in close to the rock then slowed as much as she could, wings spread, gliding on the warm updrafts. When she'd positioned herself directly under the track I let go and fell onto the saddle, the wrong way round.

'Good thing we practised this before.' I grinned, recalling my first encounter with Thoryn at Phoenix Rise.

'That's twice now I figured you were a gonner. How long you gonna keep cheatin' death?'

'Long as you're around to rescue me,' I replied. 'And now we've gotta save Yenene and fly to Phoenix Creek before this whole spirit-forsaken lump of rock breaks off.'

'What happened to Buck?'

'He's still up there. He's the high sheriff's problem now.'

We flew inland. Soaring, I saw great cracks snake their way across the baked earth as it began to break up.

We passed over Oretown. The few buildings that had been standing last time I'd visited had now all collapsed.

When we got to Phoenix Creek Yenene was nowhere to be found.

Jez flew towards me, tears streaming down her face. 'She's not here. We've searched everywhere.'

'What about her horse?'

'Gone too.'

'Perhaps she left already when she saw the quake worsening,' said the elf conductor.

'I'm not so sure, I gotta bad feeling about this.' I looked at Jez as a thought suddenly came to me. 'Jez, last time we visited, did we tell her about the Flyer not stopping at Oretown any more?'

'I can't remember but I don't think so, why?'

'What if she changed her mind?'

'Changed her mind about what?'

'The rock collapsing. What if she suddenly saw sense and wanted to leave, only she finds her horse has

268

spooked and flown off so she can't fly.'

'I know what you're thinkin'. Then she'd probably head for the station.'

'C'mon, let's go.'

Arriving at the station we saw her, a solitary figure in a black shawl, with her trunk. I breathed a huge sigh of relief. It meant she hadn't given up like part of me had feared. The fact she was even sitting there, even though no train was ever gonna whistle through the station again, gave me renewed heart. The ground was literally falling apart around her. The track bowed and buckled. She walked in circles, holding her arms up and wailing.

I yelled at her.

She looked up waving, then I realised she was waving me away. 'No, Will, go! It's too dangerous.'

'Hang on, we're coming to get you.'

Enormous cracks gaped open like jaws hungrily swallowing up whatever was on either side of them: trees, bits of platform, tangleweed, rail track, the station, the old clock tower that had never kept the right time. Then the chunk of rock the platform stood on loosed itself from its neighbours and was swept along like an iceberg of the northern shores, at the same time sinking into a dark fissure.

'Now, Shy, now!'

And Moonshine swooped with all the strength of a thunder dragon but with the agility of a windhorse, ears pricked in total concentration. She timed the dive to perfection. Alighting onto the crumbling platform Moonshine kneeled down to allow Yenene to climb onto her back, where she flung her arms around my waist, sobbing bitterly.

'A fool, I am, making you risk your life like this. What have I been thinking? It's like the scales have been lifted off my eyes and I can see how stubborn I have been. I don't know what came over me. But you and Jez shouldn't have come. You have put yourselves in danger and you've got your whole lives ahead of you.'

'We're fine, there's no way we were just gonna leave you. Everything's gonna be OK. Now, c'mon, we gotta get outta here.'

As we climbed higher to join Jez and the elf conductor there was a thunderous roar that rattled my ribcage. We all looked down as what remained of the western arm collapsed, falling outwards from the

Mid-Rock, down towards the Wastelands to be replaced by a great cloud of dust.

And the western arm, my home for fourteen years, was no more.

The ranchlands, Oretown, the bank, the sheriff's office, the hotel, miles of rail track, Pike's Ridge, part of the deep mines all scattered over the Wastelands, leaving a starkly changed landscape. A one-stem West Rock that now resembled a pruned tree, like the saddlewood Pa had cut a branch off outside my bedroom window. I choked back the tears and I knew Grandma was crying too. I felt that a chunk of me fell with it, and my heart ached like I'd never felt it ache before, except when Pa had died.

'C'mon, Shy. Take us home.'

CHAPTER FIFTEEN

★

Two Hats

I sat outside Uncle Crazy Wolf's tepee in Gung-Choux Village putting the finishing touches to my face paint – the bold red and yellow stripes of an elf brave. Sitting up on the rise in front of Chief Red Feather's tepee Jez, Yenene, Uncle Crazy Wolf (fresh out of prison) and the chief himself all sat cross-legged around the fire, waiting for me. The chief was about to commence my initiation ceremony, making me one of the tribe, at the same time giving me my new tribe name. I felt slightly nervous and a few times my trembling hands left smudges of paint on my cheeks.

It was hard to believe that just a week ago I'd been worried about saving Uncle Crazy Wolf from the gallows and Yenene from the collapsing western arm, and now my only worry was that Chief Red Feather was going to give me a ridiculous elf-brave name like Two Hats.

Things had settled down in a whole lot of ways. The rock quakes were now a thing of the past and work was already underway on connecting up the new rail track to resume the service to Deadrock and beyond. The high sheriff had begun talks over fair land treaties and some settlers were making plans to move to the Mid-Rock so there'd be more room for both ranches and elf farms on the eastern arm.

Buck was picked up by the sky cavalry fleeing along the new track that wound its way down towards Deadrock, probably hoping he could 'hole out' there for a while until the heat was off. But it wasn't to be. Within a few days, he was tried for treason and murder, found guilty, and hanged.

Amazingly Imelda had survived the fall from Thoryn's back (probably all those bandages she was wrapped in) and was now resident in Mid-Rock City jail for her part in the plot against the elf folk. Thoryn was OK too. My uncle had tended to his wounded wing with some elf healing magic. Both stone-spitters had been recovered and stored safely in Fort Mordecai.

Hox lost his job as Flyer boss and only just managed to wriggle himself out of a jail sentence. When we told the high sheriff what we'd seen that day Hox confessed that he'd instructed the troll log cutters to fell trees in the Chokewoods thinking he would eventually talk the high sheriff into letting him run a railroad through the forest. As for the stone-spitter, Hox claimed he had no idea the Gatlans planned to use it against the fort and, without proof, he was cleared of that charge.

Yenene had settled into Phoenix Rise quicker than a clattersnake's tongue. We'd only just rode into the place when she'd tutted, 'Sign's crooked, and who hung it there where you can't even see it? Needs to be higher.' Then, on seeing the barn, she'd complained. 'Barn's too small.' It still made me chuckle when I recalled Tyrone rolling his eyes, muttering, 'She's back to her old self, all right.'

'Just can't get outta the habit o' tellin' me lies, can you?' said a voice, jolting me from my thoughts. I turned round to see Yenene toss a book on the ground beside the bowl of elf paint. It was a magic book. 'Crazy

Wolf's been teaching you stuff, ain't he?'

'Grandma, who told you?' I said.

'He did,' she replied. 'Tells me you're takin' to it like a gutfish to water.'

'I was going to tell you.'

'When?'

'When I was sure it was what I wanted.'

'And is it?'

I sighed, nodding. 'It's in my blood.'

'In your blood.' She reeled. 'There are lots of things in your blood. Thought ranchin' was in your blood. Your pa was a deputy sheriff, so upholdin' the law's in your blood too.'

'Elf folk need a mage. Uncle Crazy Wolf won't live for ever. Who's gonna take over when he's gone?'

'Plenty of other young braves in the village, why does it have to be you?'

'Why are you so against me learning elf magic?'

'You know why, spirit knows I've told you often enough.'

'But that's just it, you haven't,' I said. 'Sure, you've told me that all magic has its dark side, but so does life on the Rock, so do most of the folk who live on it, especially snake-bellies. There's something you're not telling me, isn't there?'

I'd hit a nerve, I could tell. Her face went white and her lips trembled.

'You're to come now,' she said curtly. 'The ceremony's about to start.'

I followed my grandma up the hill to join the others, taking my seat, cross-legged beside the chief. Examining the long peace pipe in front of him on the ground, I sat silently, waiting for the proceedings to begin.

Kneeling by the fire, the chief lit the peace pipe but not without a few attempts. I felt my palms tingle as I thought about how I could've conjured a little pipe-lighter flame to help out. At last a thin plume of smoke rose from the bowl of the pipe and he lifted it skyward crying, 'To the Great Spirit that his wisdom remain with his people for evermore.'

That was our cue and we all said, '*Kee way soon*, the Great Spirit be with us.'

The chief passed the pipe around and we all took a puff. The smoke, which caught my eyes and made me cry, tasted horrible. And as we sat there in front of the giant totem pole, beneath the glare of the mighty thunder dragon the muscle-bound elf began to beat the drums.

When the pipe returned to him the chief cried, '*Ho, paha yatu weepee o-paha!*' which was ancient elvish for, 'Oh name-bearer bring the name.'

A procession of elf maidens wearing long-fringed dresses and leather belts decorated with colourful beadwork appeared from the chief's tepee, eyes dropped, shoulders straight, and marched slowly towards the fire. Their arms were held tight to their sides except for the last maiden who bore a long piece of wood aloft on outstretched palms.

The procession halted in front of the chief, and the name-bearer gave him the piece of wood before they all sat cross-legged on the ground directly behind him. One of the maidens smiled at me, a pretty, dark-eyed girl, and I saw Jez scowl at her.

The chief kept the piece of wood aloft and addressed me. 'Do you wish to proceed with this naming ceremony?'

'I do,' I replied.

'Carved on this tree bark are the names which have hitherto belonged to Will Gallows. In the name of the council of the Gung-Choux tribe I commit them to the fire.' At that he threw the wood into the flames. 'They are burned and go up in smoke and are known no more.'

The chief announced, 'Now I will make known the name which this council is bestowing upon Will Gallows on welcoming him as a brother and brave into our tribe.'

I held my breath, still wondering how I would come to terms with a name like Two Hats.

'Will, you are a wise warrior, and by your selfless actions to save your uncle from the hangman's noose you have delivered the tribe from annihilation at the hands of the sky cavalry, and exposed the treachery of the Gatlan brothers and other hostile ranchers. For these reasons, in the name of the council, I give to Will Gallows the elf-brave name of . . . Roaring Dragon!'

Phew! I breathed a huge sigh. I was so relieved. It was better than I could ever have hoped for.

The chief continued, 'By this honourable name, and no other, will he be known among us as long as the tribe exists. Roaring Dragon, I salute you.'

The maidens filed past and shook my hand murmuring, '*Woha*, Roaring Dragon.'

Yenene smiled. 'You done good, you are worthy of the name Roaring Dragon.'

'But not of mage?' I probed.

She sighed. 'It is your choice, son, you are no longer a child.'

My uncle came up and, putting an arm round Yenene, shook my hand vigorously. '*Woha*, Roaring Dragon. Congratulations. And you must not worry about my sister. She needs to look on you as a fine arrow: over many years she has given you wise direction but, as with an arrow, there comes a time when you must let it go.'

I noticed Yenene rolling her eyes as my uncle went on. 'She will come round to you learning the ways of a mage. We have all been through a lot, but perhaps none more than you, you saved me from the gallows rope and I will be eternally grateful. Hail, Roaring Dragon.'

'I would do it all again, Uncle Crazy Wolf. And there is something I am very grateful to you for.'

He frowned. 'There is?'

'I want to thank you for healing Thoryn.'

'Ah, our noble friend the thunder dragon. It took much healing magic but I was glad to see him fly back to his little one.' Smiling he put a hand on my shoulder. 'Will, you are welcome to stay permanently with us at the village now that you are a brave. But it is up to you.'

'Thank you, but I belong at Phoenix Rise. I might be an elf brave but I'm still a cowboy. I'd like to visit every week though to continue my mage studies – with Grandma's permission.'

Yenene nodded slowly. 'Reckon you'd sneak over anyways once my back was turned so I ain't got much choice. Still don't mean I'm happy 'bout it.'

The rest of the day was crammed with feasting and dancing then more feasting, until I figured I'd burst if I ate another thing. Then we all sat around the fire and listened to Uncle Crazy Wolf tell stories about the old elf ancestors, some of which are carved in writing and pictures on the huge totem pole in the middle of the village and which my uncle had memorised.

★ ★ ★

Later that evening we got ready to leave. I packed my things then stood at the flap of Uncle Crazy Wolf's tepee watching the sun sink lower beside the totem pole.

'*Woha*, Roaring Dragon,' said Jez walking her horse and Moonshine up to the tepee.

'Will's fine,' I replied. 'I don't really expect to be called Roaring Dragon.'

'I'm sure gonna miss everybody.' She patted Moonshine's neck. 'You too, Moonshine. Plenty of horses in Mid-Rock City but none like you.'

Moonshine, her head held high, whinnied loudly, shaking her ghostly pale mane.

'What now?' I asked Jez.

'Guess it's back to the fort kitchen. You?'

'Back to Phoenix Rise and ranch chores.'

'I know it sounds weird, and I'm glad Yenene is OK, but I'll kinda miss our trips to the western arm.'

'Me too – sort of.'

'Yenene has invited me to Phoenix Rise, but only as long as I bring some chokecherry pie.'

'You're welcome to visit anytime, Jez.'

'Make sure an' visit the fort too. And don't worry 'bout the guard, I can handle him.'

Yenene appeared riding her horse and soon we set off at a trot out of the village. We'd be riding the whole way; Yenene hated flying and it wasn't too far.

We'd only just left the village when Jez started chattering endlessly about scorpions and how she'd once been bitten by one as big as a dust rat but I didn't care, I just smiled and listened – I was only too glad to be riding back to Phoenix Rise. And with Grandma there now, it really did feel like I was going home

WILL GALLOWS ★
AND THE
SNAKE-BELLIED TROLL

DEREK KEILTY
ILLUSTRATED BY
JONNY DUDDLE

It's time for revenge!

Will Gallows, a young elfling sky cowboy, is riding out
on a dangerous quest. His mission? To bring Noose
Wormworx, the evil snake-bellied troll,
to justice. Noose is wanted for
the murder of Will's pa, and
Will won't stop until he's
got revenge!

'Wow, what a brilliant read.
Fresh and original – and
very funny too.'
Joseph Delaney, author of
The Spook's Apprentice

9781849392365 £6.99